THE PRINCESS AND THE SHEPHERD BOY

DAVID LITTLEWOOD

Copyright (C) 2021 David Littlewood

Layout design and Copyright (C) 2021 by Next Chapter

Published 2021 by Next Chapter

Edited by Icarus O'Brien - Scheffer

Cover art by CoverMint

Mass Market Paperback Edition

This book is a work of fiction. Names, characters, places, and incidents are the product of the author's imagination or are used fictitiously. Any resemblance to actual events, locales, or persons, living or dead, is purely coincidental.

All rights reserved. No part of this book may be reproduced or transmitted in any form or by any means, electronic or mechanical, including photocopying, recording, or by any information storage and retrieval system, without the author's permission.

ALSO BY DAVID LITTLEWOOD

Ghastly Gob Gissimer
Ava and the Goblin Prince
Jedrek and the Pirate Princess
Gary and the Granny-Bot

To my Grandchildren

CHAPTER 1
THE IRREGULAR PRINCESS

Princess Pollinovia shifted uncomfortably on the chair she was sitting on. True, it was a very fine chair, made especially for the princess to watch her mother's coronation as Queen. But, to a feisty young girl like Pollinovia, the whole thing seemed a frightful bore and she was getting fidgety.

Her mother, now Queen Aavantar of Universaria, looked stunning in her royal gown with all those sequins and diamonds sewn into it. And the glittering crown, which had just been placed upon her head, really topped off the whole outfit.

Everyone rejoiced at the coronation because Aavantar was believed to be the noblest Queen ever to have been crowned in Universaria. Pollinovia had heard the story again and again of how her mother had gone to rescue a people called the Omnigrots from a terrible curse put on them by an evil wizard.

The curse had transformed the once proud people into hideous goblins. But through her mother's love and duty, the curse had been lifted and they were now restored to the tall and beautiful people they once were.[1]

At Queen Aavantar's side, wearing his own crown, was her husband, King Raghan. He looked dashing and handsome—quite unlike when she had first met him, and he had been a hideous goblin. But thanks to the Queen's love and bravery, he had been transformed back into a handsome prince. Aavantar had fallen in love with him while he was still a goblin, but now his body was restored to its right form, he made a fitting husband for the new Queen.

Now, in Universaria, their customs were somewhat different from other lands of the time. While most lands had the custom of the eldest son taking the throne after the death of a king, in Universaria it was the custom that the eldest daughter became queen and her husband became king. Of course, in Aavantar's case, it didn't make much of a difference—she had no brothers or sisters anyway, as she was the only daughter of Queen Creola and King Grallion, who had ruled long and well.

Because of her heroic deeds, Aavantar had become the heroine of the people, and there had been many great celebrations in the land when her first child was born, a daughter called Mayolinthan. You might wonder why they called their daughters by such long names, but that was simply the custom of royalty in those days. Aavantar also had another daughter called Cresethame, and then a son they called Krennion. All three of them grew up perfect in the way princes and princesses are imagined to be.

However, when the last daughter came along, everyone could see there was something different about her. For a start, instead of having blue eyes and blonde hair like princesses are supposed to have, Pollinovia's hair was red and her eyes were green. She also had freckles on her face and a mischievous look. Even as a baby, she would throw the rattle out of her pram, something unheard of in a princess—in those times, anyway. As soon as she could crawl, she would chase all the royal cats and dogs around the corridors and play with her brother's toy soldiers rather than the many beautiful dolls she was given.

And—horror of horrors—when she learned to walk the princess would sneak outside and play in the mud rather than on the lush, thick carpets in the palace! She became the despair of her nurses. They gave her lots of scoldings even though they all loved her dearly. Princesses are supposed to look neat and tidy and their hair should be immaculately groomed. But Princess Pollinovia always seemed to have mud on her clothes. And her hair, no matter how the nurses combed it, had a will of its own.

One day, after a long and peaceful reign, Queen Creola passed away. There was great sadness among the people who loved their Queen, but also excitement that a new Queen, Aavantar, would ascend to the throne. King Grallion had gone into retirement after blessing his daughter, and now all that remained was to crown the new Queen.

But that is where Pollinovia (or 'Polly' as everyone called her for short - it seemed more fitting for a young scamp than 'Pollinovia') started to cause problems for those around her. She had enjoyed riding in the royal carriage and waving to the crowds that stood by the roadside, but she really wanted to get up and sit next to the driver. Her sisters and brother actually had to stop her from climbing out of the window of the carriage!

"For goodness sake, Polly," her sister, Mayolinthan had hissed. "Sit still or you'll fall out of the carriage!"

"But I want to sit by the driver!" said Polly, and by way of a protest put her face into a pout for the rest of the journey and refused her sisters' attempts to get her to wave at the crowds, as royalty are expected to do.

"Oh dear! You are such a naughty girl!" said sister Cresethame. "Just what are we going to do with you?"

Polly said nothing and buried her face in her hands.

She enjoyed the banquet that was held after her mother's coronation, despite managing to spill gravy all down the dress that had been specially made for her to wear. Then again, she didn't really like the dress as it made her feel more like a parcel than a girl. "Rotten frumpy thing!" she muttered as her nurse had struggled to fit her into it.

Now as she sat listening to the long, long speeches made by visiting dignitaries in praise of her mother, Polly shifted around more and more on the chair. She longed to go out in the palace garden and play, do some cartwheels and run around. Of course, she had been told that princesses were not supposed to behave like that—certainly her sisters would never have dreamed of turning a cartwheel or running around—but then again, Polly was not like a regular princess at all.

CHAPTER 2
THE SHEPHERD BOY

Polly was very pleased when at last all the boring speeches came to an end and she was able to slip away. She knew that the various important visitors who had come to the coronation were going to be presented to her parents, and she certainly did not want to stay for that, as she feared it would be even more boring. So, while her sisters chatted together in their usual regal manner, Polly slipped out of the great hall and made her way along the passageway which she hoped led to the garden.

The passageway was quite dark and Polly didn't really know where she was going—she had never been to the great hall before. But then she came to a turn and found that on one side there was a courtyard with a lush green lawn in the middle of it. *Just the place for running around and turning some cartwheels*, she thought.

She went out into the courtyard and saw there was a boy about her own age in the middle of it. He was a little taller than her with black hair and a tanned face that showed he spent quite a lot of time out in the sunshine. He wore servant clothes, but that was of no concern to Polly who was just glad she had found someone of her own age to talk to. Besides, the boy was holding something in his hand which intrigued her.

She walked up to him and said, "Hello! Who are you?"

"I might ask you the same question," said the boy. "I ain't seen you 'round here before."

"Huh," said Polly, wondering how this boy could have missed seeing her as a royal princess. "Don't you know who I am?"

"Yes, you're a girl!" said the boy. "No doubt one of them posh lot in there!" He pointed to the great hall. "Mind you," he laughed, "you don't look so posh with all that gravy spilt down your front!"

Princess Polly looked down on her dress with embarrassment and her face flushed bright red. "How dare you talk to me like that," she shouted, clutching her fists together.

"Well, isn't it true?" asked the boy. "You've got a right posh dress on, yet you've managed to spill gravy all down the front of it. Now, if I had posh clothes—which I haven't—I'd certainly know to treat them better than that."

"You ... you ... cheeky boy!" Polly's temper was rising fast."I've a good mind to give you a ... a ... a punch on the nose!"

The fact that Polly had never ever punched anyone on the nose and had never ever come near to doing so in her life didn't matter to her at that moment. All she wanted to do was show this cheeky boy that he shouldn't speak to a royal princess like that. Now, as a princess, she could have called the guard and had the boy arrested or something like that. But

THE PRINCESS AND THE SHEPHERD BOY

that wasn't Polly's style at all. She wanted to fight her own battles.

The boy looked at her with an amused expression. "Well, if it will make you feel better, punch away!"

"I ... I ... I'll really do it, you know," said the princess, feeling a lot less certain about punching an unknown boy on the nose.

"Well, come on then!!" The boy chuckled. "Don't keep me waiting!"

Polly, feeling she ought to make good on her threat and impose a little royal authority on the proceedings, rushed at the boy, her fists flailing. Unfortunately, the good intentions she had of bringing them home on the target of the boy's somewhat protruding nose came to nothing as the boy grabbed her arms and swung her off her feet.

"Oh!" said the princess as she sailed through the air. "Ugghhhh!" she gasped as her royal bottom landed on the grass with quite a thud and she felt all the wind knocked out of her.

She looked up at the boy who was smiling down at her.

"Hey! You've got spirit," he said. He extended his hand to her and helped Polly to her feet, where she stood trying to cover her embarrassment by brushing out her dress, which seemed to have gone all over the place. "I like you, Can't we be friends?" he asked with an appealing smile.

Polly considered this option and, as it was obvious to her that the alternative — of punching this smiling youth on the nose — was no longer possible nor indeed desirable, she decided to take him up on his offer of friendship. She wasn't sure whether a princess like herself should be friends with a common lad, but she was willing to chance it, at least that afternoon when she had no one else to talk to. After all, she could always change her mind later.

"OK," she said, "we'll be friends. But just for this afternoon!"

"You're on!" laughed the boy, his eyes smiling at her. "My name is Markus."

"I'm Polly," said the princess. It really wouldn't do, she thought, to let him know who she really was. "What's that you were holding?" she asked, pointing to the object that he had left on the ground during their brief scuffle.

"That," said Markus, picking up the object and handing it to her to look at, "is my bow."

Polly examined the object with interest. It was like a long stick—almost as long as she was tall—and it curved in the middle. A piece of twine was attached to both ends of the stick, pulled tight.

Polly stared at it. "What do you use it for?" she asked.

"Don't tell me you don't know," said Markus, surprised. "It's a bow, for shooting arrows."

"Arrows?"

"Yes. Here they are," said Markus, picking up what appeared to be a long woven basket that could be worn over a shoulder. Protruding from it were some sticks with feathers on the ends. Markus pulled one out and Polly saw that it was a wooden shaft with a point on one end and feathers on the other. Markus fitted the arrow into the bow and pulled the cord back, making the bow bend. "Watch!" he said, pointing the arrow in the direction of a tree.

Polly watched in wonder as Markus released the

arrow. It sped away and embedded itself in the tree trunk. "Wow!" she said. "Can I have a go?"

"You? You're a girl."

"So what?" said the princess.

"Girls aren't supposed to shoot arrows," said Markus.

"Why not?" demanded Polly fiercely, hands on hips. She walked up to him, hand outstretched. "Give me that!"

Markus seemed taken aback as his pretty companion snatched the bow out of his hand and proceeded to thread an arrow into it. Unfortunately, she found it more difficult than she imagined it would be. But, eventually, she pulled the arrow back and let go.

"Ow!" she exclaimed as the string snapped on her wrist and the arrow landed just in front of her.

"Not as easy as it looks, is it?" Markus grinned, obviously amused by the girl in the fancy dress trying to shoot. He picked up the arrow. "Have another try!"

Polly took the arrow and fitted it in position, then drew the bow back, pursing her lips. Markus noted the look of fierce concentration she wore as she released the arrow. This time, she did better. The arrow flew some distance before embedding itself in the ground.

"Missed again!" the princess angrily yelled.

"Come on," said Markus. "That's jolly good for a beginner!"

Polly looked at his kind smile and realised how much she liked this boy, even though she had only known him for a few minutes. Funny, but it seemed as if she had known him all her life.

"I'd better get back before I'm missed," she said.

"Can we meet again? I'd love you to teach me how to shoot."

"Sure," said Markus. "I keep my father's sheep over in the fields beyond the palace wall. I had the day off today, to see the coronation. The Queen looked wonderful!"

Polly nearly blurted out that the Queen was her mother, but she managed to restrain herself. As she walked back to join the guests at the coronation supper, she determined that she would meet the boy with the bow and arrows again.

CHAPTER 3
A LESSON IN ARCHERY

The next morning, Polly put on an old dress she used for playing in. As a princess, even an old dress was pretty fine and she wished she had something a bit less posh. Luckily, it was the day after the coronation, so there were no boring lessons for her from her tutors as everyone was clearing up after the ceremony; and the Queen herself was so tired she stayed in bed all morning.

Polly, however, was up at the crack of dawn—she wanted to go and meet her new friend with his sheep. That wasn't as easy as it sounded since princesses were not supposed to go alone outside of the palace walls. Polly did not want anyone with her, because they would likely interfere and tell her that a princess shouldn't shoot arrows. Besides, she didn't know whether people in the palace would approve of her meeting with a shepherd boy.

She went to the kitchen and gobbled up breakfast—some leftovers from yesterday's feast. There were a few servants there, but no one took notice of her, because she was often slipping in and out. As she was leaving, Polly noticed that one of the serving maids had left a headscarf and a basket on the work surface. When no one was looking, she put the headscarf around her head, placed some food into the basket, and slipped out of the door.

Polly went down the hallway and out into the courtyard. There were a couple of guards at the gates. She didn't want them to notice her, so she pulled the headscarf over her face as far as it would go, put her head down, and walked past them into the street.

"So far, so good," she murmured to herself. "Let's hope I can find him."

She felt quite nervous as it was the first time she had ventured out into the street on her own. However, she plucked up courage and went down the cobblestone street, past some rather peculiar houses on either side of the road, and through a gate which she knew led to the meadow where she hoped her shepherd boy would be.

She stared at the fields ahead, shielding her eyes from the sun. Then she saw a flock of sheep. "I wonder if it's him," she said somewhat anxiously. The flock was some way off. But, her desire to meet the shepherd boy again defeated her fear of the unknown, and she set out at a good pace towards the white fluffy figures in the distance.

The walk took longer than she anticipated as the sheep were moving in the opposite direction, but Polly walked determinedly, and within a quarter of an hour she spotted the young shepherd at the head of the flock.

"Hey! Markus!" she called out. "Markus! MAAAAAKKKKUS!" She yelled so loudly that she startled the sheep, which baa'ed and bleated.

THE PRINCESS AND THE SHEPHERD BOY

The boy turned around. "Hey!" he said, breaking into that smile which Polly found so appealing.

She ran up to him.

"I didn't think you'd come," he said.

Polly gave a pout. "Why not?" she asked.

"Because people like you don't usually mix with people like me," he replied. "But it's good to see you. My, you can shout loud for a girl!" he added with a laugh.

"Huh," said Polly, pulling a face. "Just because I'm a girl doesn't mean I can't shout!"

Markus looked at her with a mixture of fondness and amusement. "Well, you managed to put the fear of death into my sheep with your yelling. I thought they were going to run off."

Polly looked at the sheep milling about. She had never been so close to sheep before, and they made her a bit nervous, but she wasn't going to show that to the shepherd boy.

"You said you'd teach me the bow and arrow," said Polly, trying to sound authoritative.

"Oh yes," said Markus, reaching behind him and bringing his bow out. "Come on, over to that mound. We can shoot at the tree without shooting the sheep."

Polly thought it was the best time she'd ever had, chatting to the shepherd boy and learning to shoot with the bow and arrow. It certainly wasn't as easy as it looked. At the end of the morning, despite her arm aching terribly, she had learned to shoot an arrow.

"Well done!" said Markus. "But you need a lot of practice. Have you a bow and arrow at home?"

"No ... I mean ..." Polly stammered. It would never do, she reckoned, to tell the shepherd boy who she really was. "I ... I'll get my father to make one for me!"

She didn't know if her father could make a bow and arrow, but she had heard all his tales of when he was an outlaw on the run in his own kingdom[1], so she guessed he might be able to. In any case, as the King he could surely order a bow and arrow to be made for her. The only problem might be explaining to him just why she wanted one.

Then her thought process was interrupted by a loud voice behind her.

CHAPTER 4
A SUDDEN DISCOVERY

"Hey, you! Step away from the princess!"

Polly turned around to see who was hollering at her in such a fashion, and saw four very large palace guards and a man she recognised as a sergeant-at-arms from the palace in front of them. He was quite portly and very red in the face, as if he had been running hard. The sheep all started when they heard his voice. Markus moved to stop them running off.

"Stay where you are!" yelled the sergeant at Markus, as the sheep scurried around nervously. "You're under arrest!"

"Under arrest," said Markus, his face a picture of confusion. "What have I done?"

"What have you done, you young villain?" yelled the sergeant so loudly that Polly wondered whether he could ever speak in a normal voice. "Kidnapping a member of the royal family, that's what you've done."

"What?" stuttered the shepherd boy as the guards closed in on him and grabbed his arms. They then proceeded to throw Markus to the ground, face down, holding him in a vice-like grip.

"That's right, lads. Hold him tight!" bawled the sergeant. "He's obviously a very desperate character!" He picked up the bow and arrow. "We'll use this as evidence of his ill intent!"

At this point, Polly, who had watched the proceedings in dismay, thought she ought to say something: "It's all right, sergeant! I haven't been kidnapped!"

"You what, your Highness?" said the sergeant.

"He hasn't kidnapped me. I came here of my own free will to see him. Please, let him up."

The sergeant nodded to his four guards and they let Markus up. He stood dusting himself down while Polly wished the ground would open up and swallow her.

Markus stared at his young visitor: "I think you have some explaining to do! Just who are you?"

"Who is she?" asked the sergeant. Polly noticed it was the first time he had stopped shouting since he had arrived on the scene. "You young fool! Don't you know that this is Princess Pollinovia?"

Polly now wished not just the ground, but perhaps the whole earth, could swallow her up.

"Is this true?" said Markus in a wondering voice.

Polly went bright red. "Yes ... er ... it is," she stammered, looking at the ground.

"Well, I'll be ..." murmured the shepherd boy.

"All right, son," said the sergeant, patting Markus' shoulder. "It seems we were mistaken, but we've been looking for the princess for half the morning since she went missing. The whole palace guard is out searching for her." The sergeant looked at Polly and grinned. "Come on, your Highness. We must take you back. I daresay the Queen and the King have something to say to you, worrying them to death!"

"Just a minute please, sergeant," said the princess. She went up to Markus who was looking away at his sheep in a bemused and somewhat angry fashion.

"Markus," she said in a contrite way, "I'm really sorry about this. I honestly didn't mean to get you into any trouble, but I was having such a good time with you learning the bow and arrow I forgot about everything else." She looked appealingly at him. "Please say you'll continue to be my friend."

Markus looked at her. "How can a poor shepherd boy like me be the friend of a princess?"

"Of course you can," said Polly. Then, drawing herself up to her not very considerable full height, she said, "Shepherd boy, as princess I command you to be my friend and teach me the bow and arrow!"

Markus stared at her then burst out laughing. "OK," he said, "but you'll have to fix it with your mum and dad, because I sure don't want to find myself in a dungeon on account of you!"

"Don't worry," said Polly, smiling from ear to ear with happiness. "I'll talk to my parents. I dare say I'll get a real scolding for sneaking off, but I'll talk them round."

CHAPTER 5
THE SCOLDING

The first hour back at the palace was not comfortable for Princess Pollinovia. She had rightly anticipated that she would get a scolding, but it seemed that not only the Queen and King were lined up to scold her—half the palace was too!

"You naughty girl," said her nurse. "Worrying your poor mother and father like that!"

"You should have been at your studies!" said her tutor. "Mornings are for studying inside!"

"What on earth were you thinking?" said her oldest sister." Consorting with a shepherd boy!"

"I don't care whether he is a shepherd boy or not," said Polly, stamping her foot. "He is very nice and he's teaching me the bow and arrow."

"You? Learn archery?" her brother snorted. "That's not the sort of thing a princess should do."

"Why not, Krenny?" said Polly defiantly. "Are you jealous that I might get better than you?"

Prince Krennion looked wide-eyed at the King: "Father, you must speak to her!"

THE PRINCESS AND THE SHEPHERD BOY

"Leave her with us," said the Queen, and everyone left, leaving Polly alone with her mum and dad.

"Young lady," said the King, trying to be stern but failing—he seemed quite amused by his daughter's antics, "do you know what trouble you've caused?"

Polly looked at her feet and mumbled some apologies.

"The thing is, my dear," said the Queen, "you're a princess and we must know where you are."

"Did everyone know where you were when you were a princess, mother?" Polly asked innocently. She then smiled mischievously, saying, "I heard that you had adventures yourself!"

The Queen looked at her daughter with a wry smile and shook her head. "She is certainly right about that," she muttered to the King, who was smiling too. Then she looked into the fresh, appealing face of her daughter. "Polly, you have been a naughty girl, but I think we might overlook it this time."

The Queen held out her arms and she and Polly hugged another tightly. "You know," said her father, "that we should be very cross with you Polly, but you have a way of winning our hearts. But please," he added, "don't give us a scare like that again."

Polly looked at her parents. They seemed in a really good mood, so she took her opportunity to say, "I did have such a good time with the shepherd boy, learning how to shoot with the bow and arrow. He's such a nice boy and I had such a good time with him and the sheep. Can't I see him again, so he can keep teaching me?"

"I don't see why not," said the Queen with a smile. "Those shepherds are some of my most loyal subjects. I'll make arrangements."

"And can I have my own bow and arrows?" Polly said with a pleading look at her father.

"Who can resist you, you little rascal?" laughed her father. "I'll tell the bowyers[1] to make one specially for you."

"Oh, thank-you, daddy!" exclaimed Polly, her face lighting up. The princess was beside herself with joy. She couldn't wait to tell Markus the good news that she was going to see him again and learn the noble art of archery from him. What's more, she would now have her own bow and arrows to shoot with! Life looked good for the princess, but as with all things, one can never tell what lies ahead.

CHAPTER 6
A QUICK LEARNER

For the next few months, Polly was a very happy princess indeed, as she was able to go and visit her shepherd boy regularly. Of course, before she did, Markus had to go to the palace and meet the Queen. He was quite overawed by the experience, but the Queen had a gracious habit of making people—even the lowest of her subjects—feel welcome and valued. She even gave him the rare and valued drink of kallow as a treat, something he'd never tasted before. He thought it was the best drink he'd ever had.

Having made the acquaintance of the shepherd boy, the Queen then allowed her daughter to visit him. Being a princess, she wasn't allowed to go entirely on her own. A couple of the palace guards accompanied her on the orders of the King. Polly was a bit frustrated by this, but in the end she managed to persuade the guards to stand a good way off from where she and Markus were talking together.

And talk they did. Polly learned from Markus all about keeping sheep and the fun you could have with them, while he listened as she talked about life at the palace and things she found boring like lessons and sums. Not being able to read and write himself, Markus asked the princess to teach him to read in return for lessons in the bow and arrow.

This proved a very happy arrangement with two very keen pupils: Polly in the ancient art of archery, and Markus in reading and writing. To both of them, it seemed a dream come true.

King Raghan was also as good as his word at having a bow and some arrows made for his daughter. It was with great pride when she went up to Markus to show them to him. "You know," she said, "I'll now be able to practice at home—I'll soon be as good as you!"

"You do that," said Markus. "We might need them soon!"

"What do you mean?" asked the princess.

"There have been sightings of walverats," said Markus.

"Walverats?" repeated the princess. "I thought they were extinct."

"So did we," said Markus, "but some have apparently made their way in from the Dark Lands."

"Tell me about them," said Polly, cupping her chin in her hands and putting on her most inquisitive look.

"According to my father," said Markus, "they were completely exterminated in these parts, but some survived in the Dark Lands. They are a menace to shepherds, because they prey on the sheep. There have been sheep carcasses found in fields near here. That's why my father trained me with the bow and arrow—in case any come back."

"Has your father seen one?" asked the princess.

"Yes, when he was my age," said Markus. "The problem is they can attack in pairs, and have huge jaws. If you miss one, you are likely to become its dinner. That's what happened to my uncle."

"How terrible," said Polly with a grimace.

"Yes," said Markus. "Then there are the balvarets. There have been reported attacks in other districts. One flock of sheep was completely destroyed by one of these. It killed the shepherd and scattered all the sheep. Most of them were found dead of fright, or with their heads bitten off."

"We must be ready for them then!"

"We?" said Markus. "A princess mustn't get involved with things like this. I'm teaching you archery for fun. That's the understanding I've given your mother and father. It's my job to protect the sheep, not yours."

"Huh!" said Polly, unconvinced. She pouted in that way that always amused the shepherd boy and, as if to make a point, put an arrow in her bow and sent it into the tree.

"My, you are a quick learner," said Markus admiringly.

CHAPTER 7
THE ATTACK OF THE WALVERATS

Over the next year or so, Princess Pollinovia practiced hard with her bow and arrow. She even had the Queen's chief archer give her lessons and learned to shoot while riding on a horse, something Markus had never mastered, simply because he had no horse. Her best friend remained the shepherd boy, much to the dismay of her older brother and sisters.

"Polly, you're supposed to be a princess," said her older sister, Mayolinthan. "All this shooting and riding around like you do, it's not fitting."

"Why not?" asked Polly with a defiant toss of her head.

"Well, princesses are royalty and we are supposed to be dignified. All this shooting and tearing around on horses you do is not dignified at all."

"Huh!"

"And consorting with that shepherd boy."

"Well, I like him," said Polly. "He's a real friend. Besides, what do you expect me to do?"

"Well, learn the lessons your tutor gives you. And you can always read—there's the whole library."

"But the books are so boring!" sighed Polly. She knew that her sister just did not understand that, somewhere along the royal line, a spirit of adventure had crept into her. So doing lessons and reading books were not high on her list of priorities, while things like archery and horse riding were.

"Tut tut," said her elegant older sister, shaking her head and walking off in her usual regal style.

Polly had to restrain herself from sticking her tongue out at her sister's retreating back, but as she knew it would be unspeakably rude for a princess to do so, she restrained herself from the unladylike act. Besides, she was looking forward to spending the afternoon with Markus and didn't want anything to spoil it. She hadn't seen him for a bit and was longing to show him just how good she was getting at shooting.

Markus looked at her admiringly as she drew up on her horse. The feisty young maid was growing into a strong young woman with a fierce determination.

"Hello!" He smiled as she skipped off the horse. "Given the guards the slip?"

She nodded and grinned. The guards had long been left puffing behind her. She unhitched her bow and took an arrow out of the quiver[1].

"Let me show you this," began the princess, fitting an arrow to her bow, when all of a sudden there was a hideous roar and a scream of distress from the sheep. Polly looked and saw a huge creature—something like a giant hound. It had shaggy hair and huge jaws, which it was sinking into one of the terrified sheep.

"Oh no!" yelled Markus. "It's a walverat! My bow!"

He ran over to where his bow lay, but the hideous creature saw the movement and sprang at him.

Markus had no chance of reaching his weapon before the walverat was upon him, but he suddenly saw the beast stiffen and howl out in pain as an arrow thudded into its side. It raised its head to see where the missile had come from when another arrow from the princess' bow hit it in the neck. With a terrible howl, the walverat fell on its side. It thrashed around for a few seconds and then stopped moving.

Markus looked up to where Princess Pollinovia stood with her bow and another arrow threaded into it if needed. "I came to show you how well I can shoot," she said, her voice trembling a little, a shy smile on her face.

"Oh my! You certainly did that!" exclaimed the shepherd boy, his hands shaking from the shock of the encounter. "You ... You've shot the beast dead." Then he yelled, "Look out behind you!"

A terrifying growl sounded behind Polly. She whipped around to see another walverat on a mound above her, its huge jaws gaping, about to spring at her. The creature sprang, but Polly loosed her arrow at the same time, hitting the beast mid-flight, causing it to land just short of the princess. It snarled and snapped at her, but another arrow, this time from Markus' bow, hit it between the eyes, killing it at once.

With a shriek of joy, Polly embraced her shepherd boy. Of course, she had been told (especially by her older sister) that it was most improper to do this, but in the mixture of fear, relief, and elation, she felt courtly manners didn't matter very much.

"Oh, you little imp," said Markus, hugging his beloved princess tightly. "Where did you learn to shoot like that?"

"Special lessons," replied Polly, releasing herself

from his arms. She looked fondly at him. "Thank you for saving my life."

"You thank me?" gasped Markus. "If you hadn't shot that first one dead, I wouldn't have been here to save you at all. And if you hadn't put that arrow into the second walverat you'd have been dead too."

"Well, let's just say it was remarkable teamwork," said the princess, looking at the terrible creatures. "Ugh"—she shuddered—"where did they come from?"

"They come from the Dark Lands, so people say," said Markus. "Just look at those jaws!" he said, pointing at the shaggy creature lying dead on the ground.

Just then, the two guards came up puffing. "Your Highness, we can't keep up if you gallop away like that," said one of them. "Oh no!" He looked with horror at the two dead walverats. "What on earth has happened?"

"My shepherd friend and I have just killed these two horrid creatures," said Polly, trying to sound regal. "Now take them away and bury them."

"But, your Highness," stammered the guard, "what if you'd been killed? I mean, you went off without us!"

"And what would you have done if you were here?" asked the princess with a toss of her head.

"Well... we'd have...er..." stuttered the hapless guard. He stared at the two dead creatures with arrows in them. "Anyway, we gotter report this!"

"You will report that you have found two walverats shot dead," said the princess. "Nothing more!"

"But... but... what about..." stuttered the poor man.

"Why don't you just obey orders?" suggested Markus with a smile. "There's a good fellow!"

The men grumbled, but got on with what they were told to do. They pulled the hideous bodies of the walverats away and threw them into a gorge which wasn't too far away, while Polly and Markus talked earnestly together.

"I do hope my parents don't stop me coming to see you because of this," said Polly. "But we can't keep the fact of those walverats a secret."

"No," said the boy. "I hope not. Still, if you don't manage to get here, just remember that I think you're the most amazing person in the whole of Universaria!"

At which Her Royal Highness, Princess Pollinovia, blushed with embarrassment and sheer happiness.

CHAPTER 8
SOME PAINFUL INTERVIEWS

The next day, Polly woke up to find the palace alive with the news that a certain princess had killed two fierce creatures from the Dark Lands with her bow and arrow. Of course, as she suspected, the guards were unable to keep quiet about what she had done, and the news had quickly spread across the palace like wildfire. As a consequence, Polly faced several rather painful interviews.

The first was from her dear old nurse, who fussed around her as she got her ready and did her hair after she got up. "My dear Highness," spluttered the nurse, her double chins wobbling up-and-down, "running ahead of your guards like that. You could have been killed by those creatures!"

"I couldn't help that they were on foot and I was on a horse and wasn't going to wait for them. I wanted to see Markus."

"Oh, that shepherd boy! He's so much below you! You're a princess, remember?"

"I don't care about that," said Polly. "He's my best friend and I like him and don't care what he is. He's really nice, and he taught me to shoot with the bow and arrow."

"And nearly got you killed!" said the nurse gruffly.

"What do you mean?" snapped Polly, turning around and getting very heated. "It was the bow and arrow that saved my life. Without it, we would have both been dead!" She stormed to the door in dramatic fashion without waiting for the nurse to finish her hair. "I won't have that shepherd boy blamed for being kind to me! It seems as if he's the only one who understands."

The princess left the nurse with the hairbrush in her hand and a very exasperated expression on her face. "Well, I sure hope the Queen understands you better than me, missy," she said. She looked at the hairbrush and smiled. "Or maybe a few lessons in manners wouldn't come amiss? But then, you're a princess!" With that, she put the hairbrush down and got on with making the bed.

The comments that Princess Pollinovia got from her brother and sisters as she sat at the breakfast table did nothing to improve her mood.

"What on earth were you doing, putting yourself in danger?" said her oldest sister, Mayolinthan.

"Well, I didn't know there would be walverats there," said Polly.

"You shouldn't have gone in the first place! You should stay in the palace," said sister Cresethame.

"And be as dull as you, Cressy?" asked Polly with a cheeky smile.

"Oh, really!" said her sister, with an exasperated expression on her face. "And don't call me Cressy!"

"You need to learn to behave like a princess, Polly," said Prince Krennion. "I've said before that archery is not something girls should do."

"And what if I hadn't shot the arrows?" Polly raised her eyes to the ceiling. "I'd be dead along with the shepherd boy!"

"You should leave that sort of thing to the men," said her brother.

"To men like you? You couldn't hit a barn door from five paces!"

"How dare you, you little upstart!" retorted Krennion with some heat.

"Stop it, both of you!" said Princess Mayolinthan. "Mind your tongue Polly."

"I wish other people would mind theirs and stop having a go at me," said Polly, slumping in her seat. "All I did was protect myself!"

"Well, you'd better explain that to our mother," said her sister as Queen Aavantar appeared in the room. "Here she is now."

"Good morning, children!" said the Queen pleasantly as her children rose from their seats. The girls courtseyed as was the custom, and Krennion bowed his head. "I hope we're not falling out."

"Just a discussion about our sister's behaviour yesterday," said Mayolinthan as Polly's face went red.

"Ah, yes," said the Queen. "That's what I've come to talk to her about. So, if the rest of you can leave us, I can have a word with Polly on her own."

"Now you're in for it," muttered Krennion as he rose to leave. Polly resisted making a rude reply as her mother was there and as she thought she might be in enough trouble as it was.

The Queen sat down by Polly, who couldn't help

but notice how regal her mother was even without her royal robes.

"Now then, daughter," she said, "tell me exactly what happened yesterday."

Polly drew a deep, deep breath and told her mother the tale. The Queen looked at her and smiled. "Well, Polly, it appears you have been very brave and so has the shepherd boy. Did you actually shoot both those horrible creatures dead?"

"One of them, but Markus finished off the other," said Polly.

"Remarkable," murmured the Queen. "But how did he learn to shoot so well?"

"His father taught him," said Polly. "He used to be an archer."

"Hmm, I might know him," said the Queen, frowning a little. "But how come your bodyguards were not with you?"

Polly went rather red. "Err... they got ... um ... sort of left behind."

"Why?" asked the Queen.

"Well... I was on my horse."

"Really, Polly!" said the Queen. "They are there to protect you."

"Fat lot of good they'd have been against a walverat," said Polly. Then she realised she might have said the wrong thing as the Queen glared at her.

"Listen, young lady," said the Queen, "I gave you those guards for your safety. You had no right to go galloping off like that without them!"

"But I wanted more time with Markus," said the princess.

"You might have had more time with him inside a walverat's stomach," said the Queen. Then she looked at her daughter and smiled. "But I'm so proud of what you did. It was very brave."

"I must take after you, mother," said Polly, smiling back. "You had adventures too!"

"Yes, I did," mused the Queen, hugging her daughter. "But," she said somewhat stiffly, "those adventures were ordained by the Prophet Rakadan."

"Who is he?" asked Polly.

"He's someone I saw in a vision," said the Queen. "He lives on a mountain."

"Wow!" said Polly. "I'd like to meet him!"

"You might one day," said the Queen. "Now, no more of this foolishness. I don't want to quench your love of adventure, but there are these terrible creatures about and we want you safe. Or else I may have to rethink your visits to that shepherd boy."

"Yes, mother," sighed Polly.

"I'll appoint a couple of the archers to go with you," added the Queen, "in case there are other creatures around."

CHAPTER 9
POLLY SAVES THE KING

Polly was actually delighted to have the two archers accompany her when she went to see Markus. The men were, of course, experts at their craft and were able to give the two young people quite a bit of instruction whilst standing guard over them. As a result, Polly became better and better with the bow and arrow. She had a keen eye and a steady hand which enabled her to be uncannily accurate.

"Quite remarkable for a young girl," is how one of the archers put it to his companion.

"She could outshoot many men in the kingdom," said the other. He laughed. "I just hope she doesn't take our jobs. It would be embarrassing to be replaced by a princess."

As for Markus, he couldn't help but feel a little jealous the first time the princess beat him in one of the archery contests they had between themselves. Up until then, he'd always beaten her, but he now realised that this girl he had introduced to the mysteries of the bow and arrow was better than him. "I'll have to practice more just to keep up with her," he muttered to himself.

THE PRINCESS AND THE SHEPHERD BOY

As for Polly, she became quite inseparable from her bow and arrows, and insisted on taking them everywhere with her; which is why she turned up for the annual family hunt with the bow and arrows slung over her shoulder. The hunt wasn't serious, but the Queen looked on it as a family outing and an opportunity to exercise her dogs.

"Why on earth have you got those things with you, Polly?" hissed Mayolinthan. "A princess shouldn't be carrying things like that!"

"Why not?" asked Polly.

"Well ... it's not regal," said her sister.

"What's not regal about it?" asked Polly with an incredulous look.

"A princess should be a princess, not a warrior maid!" replied Mayolinthan. "It's just not done! It's not the fashion."

"Says you," said Polly. She gave a toss of her head. "Well, from now on, I intend to set a new fashion for princesses."

Just then, the Queen rode up on the black stallion that was her favourite. Polly thought how beautiful she looked. She also stared admiringly at her father, who was on a white charger.

"I hope you're not falling out again, today of all days," said the Queen, seeing Mayolinthan's obvious frustration with her younger sister.

"Polly will insist on taking her bow and arrows with her everywhere she goes," sniffed Mayolinthan. "I think it's most unladylike,"

"Well, we'll let her be less than a lady as she's your younger sister," smiled the Queen. Then to Polly, she said, "If you take those things with you, Polly, I do not want you shooting at everything. This is a hunt, not a shoot. You can take them but you are not to use them, understand?"

"Yes, mother," said Polly, making a face at her older sister when the Queen's back was turned.

"Hey, what's up?" said Krennion as he rode up with Cresethame.

"Only your little sister once again being less than a lady," said Mayolinthan.

Krennion laughed. "That's not unusual for her," he said. "What's she up to now?"

"Oh, insisting on taking her archery equipment with her," said Mayolinthan haughtily. "She should learn to carry herself like a princess."

"Something she will never do," said her brother, shaking his head. "But I wouldn't swap her for the world."

"Everyone ready?" said the Queen. "Let's go then!"

She and the King nudged their horses into action and away went the little party with the dogs and their handlers going on ahead. Polly soon felt bored by the whole thing. She liked riding, but not at this slow pace. Little did she know the excitement that was about to break upon them.

They were passing by a small wood on their right hand side, with the ground sloping away to their left. Polly and the King were riding ahead of the party as they both liked to exercise their horses at a brisk pace by riding them backwards and forwards in front of the others.

The King was riding ahead of Polly near the wood when suddenly, without warning, came a terrifying growl. This caused the King's horse to rear, throwing its rider to the ground. Polly's horse started, but as she was a little way back, she managed to regain control of it.

Out from the wood came a sight she had never seen before. A huge, black, shaggy beast, with enormous paws,- something like a bear only considerably bigger - bounded from the thicket and stood over the prostrate King with menace in its fiery eyes. Thankfully, the King was stunned by the fall and lay still while the horse bolted in terror, temporarily distracting the beast. The delay gave Polly the chance she needed.

As the beast stood on its hind legs, rearing its great height up over the body of her father, she fitted an arrow in her bow, took aim, and fired it into the monster's neck. The creature let out a hideous howl and dropped on all fours. Roaring and slavering at the mouth, it turned towards the princess and charged at her.

Polly, however, had control of her horse and already had another arrow in her bow. She took aim at the fearsome creature and, knowing there was only one shot between her and those gaping jaws, sent an arrow with uncanny accuracy into the creature's skull. The beast fell writhing to the ground as Polly steadied her horse, which by that time had become very agitated.

The rest of the party had by then reached them, including the two archers who were riding with the royal party for their protection. They had been in the back but, hearing the noise that was going on ahead of them, had ridden on and now proceeded to put a shower of arrows into the creature. The beast gave a final jerk of its huge frame and rolled over dead.

Both archers looked shocked as Polly slipped from

her horse and helped her father to his feet. The King, who had seen what happened through his dazed senses, was shaken but unhurt apart from a lump on the back of his head.

"What on earth?" he murmured as he hugged his daughter. "Polly, did I just see you shoot that thing?"

"Yes, father," said Polly. The archers looked on. It was quite touching to see the fiery young maid, who had fearlessly stood up to a terrifying creature, hugging her father like a little girl.

They walked over to where the creature was lying. The King looked at the beast, then at his daughter, and shook his head: "You saved my life, daughter of mine," he said, "but you shouldn't have put yourself in such danger."

"Well, if she hadn't, Majesty, you'd have been a goner," said one of the archers. "I never did see such skill in a young 'un, even in a boy, let alone a girl." Then realising what he'd said, he bowed and muttered, "Begging your pardon, Princess!"

The princess smiled at him. Now the rest of the party had come and there was great consternation at what had happened. They saw the beast lying dead on the ground. "Did you really shoot that thing, Polly?" asked her brother in wonder.

"Yes, but these archers finished it off," said Polly. "Good thing they were here!"

"And it's a good thing you were here first, Princess," said the second of the men. "Else we would have been too late to save your father."

"Polly! Just what have you done?" said the Queen alighting from her horse. She too hugged her daughter. "You brave, brave girl!" She looked down at where the huge creature lay. "What on earth is that? I've never seen anything like it!"

"Excuse me, Majesty," said the first one of the archers, "but I think it might be a balvaret."

"A balvaret?" said the Queen with a shocked look. "From the Dark Lands? I thought they were exterminated!"

"There have been reported sightings of them recently, Ma'am," said the archer. "They have been attacking sheep, according to what we have heard."

A flush of anger crossed the Queen's usually pleasant face. "Then why weren't the King and I told?" she asked.

"Sorry, Ma'am," said the archer. "But, according to our superiors, none of the reports were confirmed. So they didn't want to spread alarm among the people."

"Well, now we know that the reports are indeed true," said the Queen. She motioned towards the huge creature lying on the ground. "Take that thing and dispose of it," she said. "A proclamation shall be issued throughout our realm warning our people to beware of such things." She shivered. "I do hope there is not more behind this. May the Eternal Spirit help us!"

Turning then to Polly, the Queen smiled and said, "Well, young lady, you certainly have a tale to tell."

Polly nodded. She had a tale to tell. And the first person she was going to tell was a certain shepherd boy called Markus!

CHAPTER 10
THE DARK LANDS

Markus was wide-eyed with amazement when Polly told him of her adventure with the balvaret.

"Wow!" he said. "It was certainly your quick thinking and straight shooting that saved your father's life. You really are amazing!"

Polly blushed with a mixture of pride and embarrassment. She was growing so fond of the shepherd boy and wondered if it might actually be the thing they call love. She knew, of course, that it was not fitting for a princess to be in love with a shepherd boy. But then, she reasoned, her mother had loved her father when he was a goblin!

"It was nothing, really," she said, smiling shyly at him, all the while realising that it *was* really something. She had saved her father's life and killed a very dangerous creature. "But," she added, "it would never have happened without a certain shepherd boy who taught me to shoot with the bow and arrow."

It was time for Markus to blush and smile. "That was nothing," he said. "You were a good pupil. But you saved my life, and now your own father's." He looked pensively towards the hills in the distance, "I just hope the appearance of these creatures isn't the beginning of something worse."

"What do you mean?" asked the princess.

"Well, my father told me that some of the older shepherds were saying that when these creatures appear, it means there is a threat from the Dark Lands."

"Just what are the Dark Lands?"

"They are the lands where all sorts of evil exist. They sometimes invade parts of our lands, then they have to be dealt with. Apparently, your own mother conquered an evil wizard from there when she was young."

"She was so brave. We're very proud of her for that!"

"I'm sure at least one of her daughters takes after her."

Polly blushed. "I only did what anyone else would have done."

"I don't think many girls would have faced those beasts like you did," said Markus. He looked at her seriously. "I just hope we don't have to face them again!"

"You think we may?" said Polly, her face turning serious.

"Who knows what the future holds," said her shepherd boy with a shake of his head. "But it will always be better with you around."

Polly returned home in a thoughtful mood. When she got to the palace, she went to see her mother. "Just what are the Dark Lands mother?" she asked.

The Queen looked somewhat uneasy. "Why do you ask such a question?"

"People say we could be facing a threat from

them. They say that the creatures we killed come from there."

"Believe me, my child," said the Queen with a pained expression, "the Dark Lands are where all manner of terrible creatures dwell. They are creatures under the power of evil wizards and magicians who live there and who use them to invade lands where there is the light of the Eternal Spirit." She sighed. "No good dwells in the Dark Lands. All is evil."

"Are they a threat to us, mother?" asked Polly. "Are they likely to try to invade us?"

"That we cannot tell," said the Queen, "but we must certainly be ready for anything. I have instructed the army to be in a state of full alert." She smiled at her daughter and said, "But for now you must not concern yourself with such things. You have so much growing up to do!"

Polly hugged her mother before the Queen left the room, but was left distinctly uneasy by their conversation. Was it possible that some creatures from the Dark Lands were about to invade? As she went into her bedroom she looked at her bow and the quiver of arrows lying on the chair. If there was an invasion, she thought, then this princess would certainly be ready for them.

CHAPTER 11
THE FLYING BED

Polly went to bed that night just as she had always done every day of her young life. As usual, her nurse fussed about her, but the fussing seemed to get on Polly's nerves more than usual. She even snapped at her nurse, which really upset the poor old thing, and Polly was relieved when she was left alone, tucked up in bed.

"Sorry, Nursey," she said as her elderly companion left the room. "I was mean to you."

"Don't worry, my dear," said the nurse. "You're tired out. Just get some sleep."

Polly turned over in bed and gazed into the darkness of her room. She had asked the nurse to leave her curtains open as it was a moonlit night and Polly loved going to sleep with moonlight shining through the window. The princess sighed contentedly as she snuggled her head into the soft pillow of her bed. No matter what was happening in the Dark Lands, it all felt so peaceful here. She wondered what her beloved shepherd boy was doing as she drifted into a welcome slumber.

Polly's slumber, however, was about to be interrupted. She gave a start as she felt the bed trembling under her, then a little cry of alarm as it lifted off the floor with her in it and headed upwards towards the ceiling! Polly screamed out loud as she saw the ceiling rush towards her, certain she would be crushed to death on it.

But just as she reached it, the ceiling seemed to melt away and Polly found herself flying over the rooftops. She hung on to her bed as it swayed about in the wind and then lurched away at great speed towards the moon.

"What on earth is happening," she exclaimed. "I'm on a flying bed. This just can't be happening. I must be dreaming!"

By now Polly realised she was up above the clouds. She saw them like specks of white cotton wool below her. Above her she saw the stars as she had never seen them before, so bright and shiny they appeared just as if someone had let off a firework display in the heavens. Her fear gave way to a feeling of exhilaration. "Whatever is happening it is sure exciting," she murmured to herself.

Suddenly, Polly caught her breath as the bed suddenly dipped downwards. If you have ever been on a roller coaster you will know how she felt as her stomach disappeared from inside her.

Down below, she saw a range of mountains. The bed appeared to be heading straight towards one of them and she noticed that this particular mountain had a golden top to it which was glistening in the moonlight. Now, Polly had seen plenty of gold in the palace, but had never seen a mountain made of it. Down and down went the bed at high speed. Polly gasped, wondering how on earth she would survive the landing. She shut her eyes in anticipation of the crash, but the bed, instead of being smashed to pieces on the mountain, simply landed with a small bump with the princess still safely tucked in.

"Wow! That was some ride!" said Polly as she looked around her. Where was she? Glancing around in the moonlight, which seemed far stronger here, she saw what looked like an old, broken down hut made of wood and plaster. It appeared to be the only building around and Polly thought it looked very much out of place on this golden summit.

However, it brought to her mind a story her mother had told her about a rickety hut on a golden summit in which lived an old, old man with strange and wonderful powers. Could this be the same summit and the same old man? There was only one way to find out. The princess noticed there was smoke coming from the rickety chimney and decided there must be someone inside. So she gathered her courage, stepped off the bed, and walked towards the hut. One strange thing she noticed was that as she came nearer the hut appeared to be larger than she first thought. Larger and larger it grew until it was almost a small house.

"Mother did tell me about this place, I'm sure," said Polly to herself. "Oh well, let's see if anyone's in!"

She walked up to the door. It was a very old door held together with an iron frame. Polly saw there were cracks in the wood so that she could just make out the outline of the room inside and a fire in the grate. She drew a deep, deep breath and knocked on the door.

"Come in," said a deep voice from inside.

CHAPTER 12
WHAT THE PROPHET SAID

Polly turned the handle on the door and found herself inside a room which had a window in the roof through which the moonlight was streaming, bathing the room in light. She looked in wonder as she saw the moonbeams dancing off a line of golden drinking goblets that hung from a shelf on one of the walls. She stared at them and saw it was as if they were alive and dancing with joy. In fact, the whole room seemed to give off a sense of joy and wonder. She could almost hear it singing as the moonbeams flitted around.

There's certainly magic here, thought Polly as she looked at the fire burning in the hearth. She noticed that the flames did not look like ordinary flames, but were actually in the shape of people and animals dancing in the grate. They seemed to be dancing to music which, although she could not see any instruments playing, appeared to be coming from all parts of the room.

"Welcome, my child," said a deep voice. Polly looked and there was a very old man with a bald head and a very long white beard sitting at a wooden table in the middle of the room. On the table were all sorts of scrolls and parchments, quills and ink bottles. It appeared that the old man - whoever he was - did plenty of writing.

Polly stared at him. She noticed his beard was so long it brushed the floor. And although he was obviously very old, his face shone with a radiance that made him look young and old at the same time. He was very thin and wore a tunic which appeared to be made of coarse brown cloth. *Just like a sack,* thought Polly.

The old man stared at Polly with eyes that were warm yet penetrating at the same time. "So you are Princess Pollinovia, daughter of Queen Aavantar," he said. "Welcome, Chosen One!"

"Chosen One!" said Polly in wonderment. "Chosen for what?" She glanced around the room: "Why am I here? And who are you?"

"I am the Prophet Rakadan," said the old man with a slight bow.

"The Prophet Rakadan who my mother told me about?"

"The same!"

"But ... what do you want with me?"

"I have summoned you here because the Eternal Spirit has chosen you to be the champion of your people."

"The champion of my people?" said Polly with an amazed look on her face. "But why should my people need a champion, and why on earth should it be me?"

"There is coming a time of great danger to your people," said Rakadan. "There are plans and activities afoot in the Dark Lands to invade and take over your country."

Polly looked alarmed. "Oh no!" she exclaimed, putting her hand to her mouth. "I've heard about the Dark Lands. All sorts of horrid creatures live there, don't they?"

"Yes, and very evil ones too. They are bent on enslaving and destroying your people."

"But we are so happy in our country. Why would they want to do that?"

The Prophet sighed. "There is no telling the extent and destructiveness of evil, my child. Evil cannot have any part of goodness or happiness, so it tries to destroy those things which are good and happy. It is the purpose of evil to enslave the things which are good."

"Are they going to come and make us slaves, then? Even my mum and dad?"

"That is their intention," said the Prophet gravely. "However, I have a plan to prevent them from carrying out their evil scheme."

"But who are they?" asked Polly. "What are they called?"

"They are the Nephilites," said Rakadan. "They are an evil race. They spring from a race of giants who invaded and occupied a neighbouring country and then mixed with the inhabitants. Sadly, the evil in them came through in the generations of mutants that followed."

"So, are they all big?" asked Polly.

"They are all about twice the size of most of your people. Their king is huge. He has had an enormous iron bedstead made for him in the Dark Lands."

"How do they live? What do they do?" asked Polly.

"They are all bandits. They make their living by

trading in the slaves whom they capture from surrounding countries. Now they are looking further afield for prey and plunder."

"And we are next on their list?"

"Yes, they have plans laid up for invasion."

"How will they come?" asked Polly.

"They come in on chariots drawn by huge creatures called nanors. They can travel very fast on raids. They also have a sort of cavalry which is mounted on flying giant bats called regats. Let me show you. Watch carefully!"

The Prophet reached over to an earthenware jar from which he took some white powder. He threw the powder on the fire and a huge cloud of mist billowed up in the room. As Polly stared at it, she could make out figures moving around in the dust cloud, figures like men, only very tall with terrible, cruel faces. They carried spears and battle axes, and appeared to be covered in scales, like fish. She could see some of them riding in chariots drawn by large, ugly creatures on four legs, like giant lizards. She guessed these must be the nanors Rakadan told her about.

"Oh no!" said Polly. "How can we stop them?"

"Naturally speaking, it is impossible," said Rakadan with a grave shake of his head. "But the Eternal Spirit ordained me as guardian of your lands, so I have obtained weapons for you."

Polly gave a little gasp. "Weapons ... for me?"

"If you are to be the champion of your people, you will need them."

"*ME?*" said Polly incredulously. "Me, a champion of my people? I'm just a young girl."

"In the realm of the Eternal Spirit the race is not

always to the strong, my child," said the old man. "In his kingdom the weak confound the strong."

"Why? How?" said Polly, her eyes opened wide.

"It is the custom of the King of the Nephilites to challenge the champion of the country they are invading, to armed combat. The winner takes the kingdom." The Prophet gestured towards the fireplace where an enormous figure appeared. "As you see, he is very big and very fierce, so most of the time no-one will fight him. If they do, they are very quickly beaten."

"You don't mean ... you're not saying ... I should fight this creature?" Polly's mouth hung open. "How on earth could I do that? He'd tear me to pieces in a few seconds! Besides, he has those awful weapons. What do I have?"

The old man smiled. "You have a good heart and the ability to shoot straight. They are what you will need to handle the weapons I give you."

"Weapons? What weapons?"

Rakadan gestured to the fireplace and the mist cleared. He stood up and walked over with a rather bent back to the wall. Polly noticed that, hanging on hooks on the wall, were a sword, a bow, and some arrows. The Prophet reached up and took them off the wall, then came over to where Polly was sitting. "These will be your weapons, Princess," he said, putting them in front of her. "With them, you will overcome the evil ones."

"A sword and a bow and arrows?" said Polly. "Against that great monster?"

"They are the arrows of faith and the sword of truth blessed by the Eternal Spirit," said Rakadan. "With them you will defeat the enemy and save your people."

"But there are only five arrows here," said Polly, examining what Rakadan put in front of her. "They won't last long against an army."

"As long as they are used for good in faith there will always be five there. That is the number willed by the Eternal Spirit."

Weird, thought Polly without saying anything. She pulled one of the arrows out and saw it was bright red. It glistened in the moonlight and seemed to radiate a strange power. *Almost as if it's alive*, thought the princess.

"Each arrow is packed with power to destroy those things that are evil," said the Prophet as if reading Polly's thoughts. "Shoot straight and true into the heart of evil. Now, look at the sword."

"I can't use a sword very well," said Polly as she pulled the sword out of its scabbard. "Oh!" she exclaimed as the sword began to glow.

"The sword will fight for you," said Rakadan. "Every time you hold it up. Brandish it!"

Polly held the sword in the air and light flashed from it. "The truth will blind every enemy," said Rakadan. "They will not be able to stand before you. Now kneel before me. Your time here is nearly at an end."

Polly knelt before the little old man. He took a small flask of oil from the table and poured it over the princess' head. "I anoint you in the name of the Eternal Spirit." said Rakadan, laying his hands on her head. "Now go in the strength of that name and be the champion of your people!"

Polly gasped as she felt a strange power creeping all over her. She had never felt so happy yet so brave in all her life. She closed her eyes and fell into a deep sleep.

When she woke up, she was back in her bedroom lying on her bed. Morning was breaking through the window.

"What a strange dream," she said as she yawned and sat up. "Almost as if it was real."

Then she started as she saw what was at the foot of her bed. "Oh!" she exclaimed as saw lying there the sword of truth and the arrows of faith — the very ones the Prophet had given her.

"So, it wasn't a dream after all," said Polly to herself. "I'm sure now that Prophet Rakadan is the same one who met my mother. I wonder what the future has in store."

That future was about to be revealed as Polly heard running steps and voices outside the door.

CHAPTER 13
THE INVASION OF THE NEPHILITES

The first Polly heard of it was when her nurse burst into the room looking more flustered and red-faced than usual. "Your Highness, you must get up immediately," she exclaimed breathlessly, as if she had been running. "The Queen is putting everyone on an emergency alert!"

"Emergency alert?" said Polly. "What on earth is that?"

"There has been an invasion, your Highness," said the nurse with a despairing look. "We have been invaded!"

"Invaded? By whom?"

"There is a terrible army from the Dark Lands," sobbed the nurse. "Oh, that I should ever see this day!"

"Now, now, Nursey!" said the princess in spite of her alarm. "I'm sure my mother will have a plan!"

"I do hope so," said the nurse, wringing her hands. "She is so wise."

"I'm sure," said Polly. She loved her nurse but she had found her a real old fusspot lately. "Now, for goodness sake, let's hurry up and get me dressed!"

Polly dressed in a hurry despite the fussing of the

nurse, and hurried down to her mother's room to see what was happening. When she got there, she discovered that her mother was meeting with the King and her advisors about the crisis that had arisen. So Polly had to be content with finding out more from her sisters and brother.

"Just what is happening?" she asked Princess Mayolinthan.

"It's unclear at the moment," said her older sister, "but we think that there has been an invasion from the north by a tribe from the Dark Lands." She looked worried. "They say it's a very serious situation."

"They say they want to make us slaves," said her other sister, Princess Cresethame, looking rather pale.

"Which means we will have to go and fight to defend our lands," said Prince Krennion gallantly. "Father is marshalling the troops at the moment, and I shall be among them," he said, drawing an imaginary sword.

"So shall I," piped up Polly, who then wished she hadn't spoken as every eye turned upon her.

"You!" said Krennion. "You can't go. This is for men, not little girls."

"I'm not a little girl," snapped Polly, shoving her face into that of her brother's, "and what's more, you'll need everyone who can shoot an arrow straight."

"But this is war, and war is not for girls!" protested her brother.

"Why not?" asked Polly with a toss of her head.

"Polly, girls don't fight in wars," said Cresethame. "It just isn't done. I do wish that you wouldn't get these silly ideas."

"We'll see about that," said Polly as she stuck her nose in the air defiantly and headed for the door. Her

THE PRINCESS AND THE SHEPHERD BOY

way, however, was blocked by a rather large footman who announced the entrance of the Queen. Polly's brother and sisters smiled at her performance as she bounced off the footman and sat on the floor. "Ugh!" she said.

"Your Highness, I am so sorry," said the footman, quite aghast that he'd knocked the young princess over.

"You needn't be," said her brother. "She just wasn't watching where she was going, as usual." Then turning to Polly, who had just got up quite winded, he said, "You see, Polly—if a footman can knock you over, that's how you'll end up in a battle!"

"Now, what's all this, children?" asked the Queen. "I hope you're not all arguing again at a time like this."

"Just trying to persuade my little sister that war is not a game for girls," said Krennion rather haughtily.

"Indeed, it is not a game," said the Queen gravely. "I am afraid, children, we are all in great danger."

"Where from?" gasped Mayolinthan.

"There's a band of invaders who have come from the Dark Lands," said the Queen. "They have taken some prisoners already. It's thought that they've come to make us all slaves."

"Oh no!" Cresethame's eyes filled with tears. "I don't want to be a slave!"

"That's why your brave father has led out the army to stop them," said the Queen. "I have just received a message that the two armies are camped a short distance from here."

"Have they stopped the advance?" said Krennion.

"Yes, but their king has apparently challenged your father to hand-to-hand combat." said the Queen with a worried look. "The winner will take the kingdom."

"Father is a great warrior," said Krennion. "I've heard his stories."

"Yes, but that was a long time ago," said the Queen. "He's older now, and we've had peace here for so long that everyone is out of practice."

"Well, I'm not," said Polly. "I'll go and help father!"

"Here we go again," said Krennion.

"Polly, don't say such silly things at a time like this," said the Queen rather sternly. "It's not helpful."

"We've been trying to tell her that," said the prince with a sigh.

"You shut up!" said Polly, with tears in her eyes.

"Polly, that's very rude," said the Queen. "Go to your room at once!"

"But ... but ..." stammered Polly.

"Go to your room. Now!"

Polly burst into tears and fled from the room. This was awful. She had thought she was going to be the saviour of her family and her people, but no one seemed to understand. As it was, all she had done was cause a family argument. She ran to her room, slammed the door behind her, and fell on the bed sobbing her heart out.

CHAPTER 14
WAR

Later that morning, Prince Krennion went off to join his father in the war. Polly was still miffed with him, but she came out of her room to see him off and wish him well. As she did so, she suddenly realised how much she loved her brother and was dreadfully afraid in case anything happened to him. She thought of the sword and the arrows Rakadan had given her and wondered what she should do.

So, she slipped unnoticed out of the palace and went off to see her best friend, Markus. The shepherd boy was as yet too young to go off to the war, but he was practising his skills as an archer when Polly found him.

"Hi," said Markus, his face creasing in the smile Polly always found irresistible. "What are you looking so down in the mouth about?"

"Haven't you heard what's happening?" asked Polly quite fiercely. "How can you be so complacent?"

"Well, I can't see how it would help being miserable about things," replied the shepherd boy. "If you think that going around with a face as long as a wet weekend will help matters, then I'll look as miserable as you!"

"How ... how dare you!" snapped Polly. "Have you forgotten who I am?"

"No, you're a spoilt brat of a princess who happens to be my friend."

Polly looked daggers at him, then suddenly saw the humour in what he said and laughed. "Oh, I do like you!" she said. "I like you because you're the only person who doesn't treat me like a princess."

"Well, perhaps I'm the one with the most sense," said Markus. "You're an awesome friend, princess or not, so I want to keep it that way."

Polly looked at her shepherd boy and felt again the stirrings of ... was it again the thing they called love? All she did know at that moment was she wanted to put her arms around him and kiss him, but she knew that would not be proper. So, she decided to tell him what she had come for.

"Actually, I've come to talk to you as a friend," she said. "I think you're the only person who should know."

"What's this—a terrible secret?" said Markus.

Polly drew a deep, deep, breath. "Last night, something incredible happened," she began. "You really aren't going to believe this, but it's true. I swear it."

"Well, go on—tell me! I can see it's important."

Polly hesitated. "I think you're the only person who won't think I'm crazy." Then she drew another deep breath and launched into telling her shepherd friend about everything that had happened the previous night. She told him about the flying bed, the golden mountain, the Prophet Rakadan and the sword and the arrows he had given her.

Markus' eyes opened wide at the tale. "Polly, are you sure this wasn't a dream?"

"No, it wasn't!" Polly stamped her foot. "I knew you wouldn't believe me."

Markus sighed. "It does sound a bit incredible to me. Do you mean to say that this Prophet has told you to face this monster? How on earth can this be right?"

"Through the sword and arrows Rakadan has given me. I have faith in them!"

"But you're just a girl," said Markus.

"That's what everyone says," said Polly crossly. "But I can shoot as well as anyone, and with the arrows of faith Rakadan gave me, I will beat him."

"Do you really think so?"

"Remember that walverat?" asked Polly. "It was going to kill us, but we shot it dead. And the balvaret? Shot dead too. And by the help of the Eternal Spirit and the weapons the Prophet gave me this dreadful Nephilite king will go the same way!"

She looked at Markus appealingly. "I'm going off to the battle. Will you come with me?"

"Me?" said Markus. "What could I do?"

"You could be my armour bearer," said the princess. "And my friend."

"I've heard of some mad ideas," said Markus, scratching his head, "but this is really the maddest I've ever heard. I mean, two kids going off to battle."

"If you won't go with me, I'll go on my own," snapped Polly.

"All right then," said Markus. "I daresay we will get into all sorts of trouble. How will we get there? Have you thought of that?"

"We'll ride," said Polly. "I can borrow a horse for you."

"But I can't ride," said the shepherd boy. "I've never sat on a horse."

"In that case, I will take my horse and you can sit behind me and hold on," said Polly.

"Great!" murmured Markus to himself, without enthusiasm.

"We ride first light tomorrow," said Polly. "Be ready!"

"Yes, Ma'am!" said the shepherd boy, smiling and making a mock bow. "I am at your Highness' command!"

Not knowing what to do in the light of his gentle mockery, Polly stuck her tongue out at him, then departed. As she went, she realised it was a thing most unbecoming of a princess to do to one of her subjects, but she didn't care. All she knew was she was becoming uncommonly fond of the shepherd boy.

CHAPTER 15
OFF TO BATTLE

The next morning, Polly rose early, before it was light. She put on a shirt and a jacket with trousers she'd borrowed from one of the servant boys. It wasn't what princesses usually wore, but most princesses, she reasoned, were not going to war. She pulled on a pair of boots she used for riding, then picked up the bow and the precious faith arrows she had been given by the Prophet. Polly took one of them out and stared at it in the semi-darkness of the room. It glistened bright and red, almost as if something was glowing inside the shaft. She reached for the sword that was lying at the foot of the bed. As she touched it, a flash of light came from it and made her jump.

"These things are almost alive," she said to herself as she strapped the sword around her waist. It was just the right size for her. "Made to measure, just for me," she said proudly.

Trying to hide herself in the shadows, Polly crept to the stable where her horse was waiting. Thankfully, the grooms were all asleep, as the hour was early, so there was no-one about as she saddled her beautiful chestnut steed and mounted it. She leaned down and whispered in the horse's ear, "Come on, Chessy! We have work to do!"

The horse trotted out into the yard. Polly saw the dawn starting to break and knew she had to get going. She drew a deep breath. "Here we go," she said. "May Rakadan and the Eternal Spirit be with us!"

Polly galloped her horse until she reached the place she had arranged to meet Markus at. He was there waiting for her with a somewhat anxious look on his face.

"Climb on," said Polly. "Hurry up. I don't want anyone sending search parties out for us."

Markus climbed up uncertainly on to the back of the horse, and Polly trotted them out down the road.

"Hold tight," giggled the princess, liking the feeling of the shepherd boy's arms around her waist, and liking it even more when he held on tighter. "Don't be nervous."

"Please excuse me if I'm sick," muttered Markus in her ear, as the horse jolted him up and down.

"Hang on," said the princess as she stuck her heels into the horse and it sped along at a brisk trot. Markus groaned and dutifully hung on to his princess.

"You're doing this deliberately, aren't you?" he said.

After riding for an hour, they dismounted to rest the horse, and also eat and drink some of the provisions from the kitchen that Polly had brought with her. Markus moaned that he never felt so stiff and sore in his life but, after they finished their meal, he gamely climbed on for the rest of the journey. They trotted along past fields and hedgerows, past old buildings which acted as markers for the path, until finally they saw in the distance what appeared to be a set of mirrors, but turned out to be armour gleaming in the sun.

Polly shielded her eyes from the glare as she approached her father's army. They were drawn up in ranks opposite all sorts of weird creatures, with many huge, giant figures among them. She guessed that these were the Nephilites, the enemy invaders. As she drew nearer, she noticed other strange creatures flying overhead, just like bats. *They must be the regats,* thought Polly.

As she looked at the size of the opposing army, she realised that her father's army would have no chance against such a force; the only hope her countrymen had lay in her defeating the Nephilite King in answer to his challenge, if and when it came. If she didn't, her people would be enslaved or wiped from the earth by these terrible creatures.

A voice came from behind her. "Wow! Look at that lot! We don't stand a chance!"

"Hold your tongue, Markus," said the princess as a strange power crept over her. It was the same power she had felt when the Prophet had poured oil on her. "There are more of us than there are of them!"

"I don't see it," muttered Markus, rather hurt by the sharp rebuke.

"That's because you cannot see into the power of the Eternal Spirit!" declared Polly, surprised at her own words. "His power is with us and it is more than all those foul fiends."

"I hope you're right," said the shepherd boy. "Otherwise, we're all going to end up as slaves if they don't kill us first."

"Not if I can help it," said Polly. "Come on, Chessy. You've done well!"

She urged the tired horse to the edge of the camp where they dismounted. They looked at the soldiers, who were carrying weapons and wearing light armour. They were all looking very grave and seemed to be dreading the battle that was to come. The soldiers stared at Polly quite curiously, but Polly did not stay to talk to them. She just hoped that no-one would recognise her, for she knew if the King heard she was there, he would send her straight back to the palace. He would never allow her to take part in the battle, let alone fight the Nephilite King.

Just then, there was the sound of a trumpet and a stir in the ranks of the army.

"It's him again!" said one of the soldiers.

CHAPTER 16
THE CHALLENGE

Polly and Markus pushed their way to the front of the line of soldiers. What they saw took their breath away. Coming from the ranks of the Nephilites opposite them was a huge chariot. It had long, evil looking knives on the wheels and was drawn by two extraordinary creatures. They were about the size of horses but were green with fish-like scales, and had heads like giant lizards. Polly guessed rightly that these were the nanors she had seen at Rakadan's hearth. *They look fierce enough to frighten anyone*, she thought, as a shiver went down her spine.

Standing in the chariot, holding the reins that were attached to the creatures, was a huge, ugly figure. Polly reckoned he must have been at least five metres tall and standing in the chariot made him appear even bigger. He was a curious creature in that, although he was shaped like a human being, he was covered in scales which made him look like he was wearing a suit of armour. It was quite obvious to Polly that it would take a very forceful shot from an arrow to pierce those scales. She also noticed he held an enormous curved sword in his right hand.

As for his face, it was hideous in its cruelty. He had a black beard and a mop of hair to match, through which two red eyes poked out. His ears were pointed and his enormous red nose was shaped in a sharp hook which stuck out from his beard. *Rather like a bent carrot,* thought Polly.

"No way we can match that monster," said Markus, clutching his bow. "My arrows would bounce off."

"If you're scared, go home," hissed Polly.

Markus was in fact scared to bits, but there was no way he was going to admit that to Polly. Besides, he reasoned that it would be better to fight these monsters and die, rather than be their slaves. What he doubted was what a young princess and a shepherd boy could do in the face of such odds. But he put his fears to one side and spoke boldly in Polly's ear. "I'm right behind you, Princess."

"Good!" said Polly. "Listen—I think that awful creature is going to speak."

The huge figure stepped out of the chariot, sheathed his sword and stood with his hands on his hips in a defiant pose. He lifted his head and boomed out in a loud voice: "I am Caspage, King of the Nephilites. I have won my crown by armed combat. I fight and kill all who fight me and now I am challenging you."

The giant paused and cleared his throat. "It is easy for us to conquer weak, helpless people like you, as we are all warriors trained to kill," he said with a horrible smirk. "But I like sport, so I am issuing a sporting challenge to you. Get your best man to fight me. If I win, which I will, you become our slaves. If your man wins, then we return to where we came from. Of course," he continued with a laugh that creased his cruel face, "there is no chance of him beating me. But I like a bit of sport, so send someone now!"

He paused and turned to the band of giant figures behind him who cheered him to the echo, filling the air with hideous cries and bloodcurdling howls. Suddenly, Polly noticed two creatures rise into the air and fly around like huge bats. They had long claws which hung down. As she stared, she saw there was a figure mounted on each one, not as tall as a Nephilite but equally hideous.

They must be the regats Rakadan told me about, thought Polly. *Thank goodness there are only two of them.*

"Come on," said King Caspage. "Who will be man enough to face me? Or are you all a bunch of lily-livered cowards afraid to fight?" He lifted his ugly head. "I defy you all!" he bellowed as the cheering rose behind him again. "I defy your king and country!"

Polly looked at the soldiers standing around her. They were obviously terrified by the Nephilite's speech. She realised that she would have no help from them.

Suddenly a strange boldness came upon her—it was the same boldness she had felt at the Prophet's house when he poured the oil over her. She somehow knew the time had come to act and put her weapons to the test.

"Come on!" she said to Markus. "Let's go get him!"

CHAPTER 17
THE FIGHT

Polly slipped through the lines of soldiers and walked into the space between the armies with Markus loyally following her. He didn't feel any of her courage and was actually scared silly by the whole thing. But then, being brave is feeling fear and doing it anyway. Even if it was a suicide mission — and it looked very much like it would be one — he was going to stick by his princess.

Polly's sudden appearance caused a great stirring and murmuring in the ranks of her own army. "Look, it's the princess!" and "What's she doing here?" went through the line of soldiers. Someone ran to tell the King what was happening and he and Prince Krennion rushed out to see Princess Pollinovia and a shepherd boy facing up to the huge giant.

Caspage saw them coming and glowered at them. "What's this," he roared, "children coming out to fight me? Can't you do any better than that?"

"Polly, come back before it's too late," called out the King despairingly. He wondered just what mad idea had gotten into his daughter, and dreaded seeing her torn to pieces by the monster.

Polly, however, had no sense of fear of the giant. She was trusting implicitly in the weapons that the Prophet had given her. She called out to the giant: "You make a lot of noise, King Caspage. But today, you will be silenced forever."

Caspage stared at her with a look of pure hatred. "By you?" he said contemptuously. "A mere slip of a girl and a weak looking boy? Why, I'll tear you both to pieces with one hand and roast your remains over a fire."

"You come with your swords and chariots to enslave my people," said Polly, "but I come to you in the name of the Eternal Spirit and the Prophet Rakadan. I have weapons which will destroy you and your army. So I am giving you the chance to clear off now and leave us forever while you still have a chance."

"What?" said the giant in amazement, drawing himself up to his full, terrifying height. "Do you know who I am?"

"You are King Caspage," said Polly, amazed at the boldness of the words coming out of her mouth, "who makes himself fat by enslaving innocent people. You are a bandit and a robber, but today your wickedness is coming to an end. Now, are you going to fight or get out of our lands?"

"You impudent young puppy!" roared the giant. "Prepare to die!"

The giant took out his huge curved sword and started to take massive strides towards where Polly and Markus were standing. The King and Prince Krennion looked in dismay as the giant thundered down the ground to kill their beloved Polly. But Polly had drawn one of the arrows of faith out of its quiver and fitted it into her bow. She looked down the shaft as the arrow glowed brightly with a supernatural light, which even showed up in the morning sunlight.

"In the name of the Eternal Spirit," she said, "Rakadan guide my arrow."

With that, Polly released the arrow straight at the onrushing giant. She knew she would only have one shot before the giant was upon her and had no idea what the arrow would actually do.

She watched wonderingly as the arrow burst into flames as it left her bow. Gathering speed, it hurtled towards the giant, whose warlike look suddenly turned to horror as he saw what was coming at him. He had been shot at by arrows many times before, and they had simply bounced off. But this was something different.

Polly's shot was straight and true. The flaming arrow hit the giant in the chest with an enormous explosion. There was a huge flash and a great billow of smoke rose up. When the smoke cleared, there was no sign of the giant. All that was left of him was a pile of dust on the grass.

"Wow!" said Markus, jumping up and down with excitement. "Whatever that Prophet put into those arrows sure was potent!" He suddenly pointed upwards and said, "Look out, Polly! Above you!"

Polly glanced up to see two of the terrible regats and their riders bearing down on them. She quickly fitted another arrow and shot it at one of them. Again, the arrow took off like a flaming missile which the regat tried in vain to avoid. There was another enormous explosion and the regat and its rider were no more. However, at that instance, Polly heard Markus cry out as the other regat seized him in its terrible claws and made off with him. Polly fitted another arrow into her bow but knew she couldn't risk shooting the regat as she would undoubtedly kill Markus too.

However, there was much more to occupy her mind at that moment. A cry went up in the ranks of the Nephilites: "They have killed our king! Destroy them! Forward!"

Polly saw the whole ranks of the terrible army move forward towards them. There were the huge giants, some with chariots drawn by nanors, whose wheels would deal her troops a lethal blow. Then there were other creatures, smaller but equally fierce and armed to the teeth with battle axes, swords, and spears. King Rhagan ordered his archers to fire, but the arrows seemed to bounce off. Polly took another arrow out of its quiver and fired it at the onrushing hoard. There was again a huge explosion and a gap in the ranks, but not enough to stop the evil army who were hellbent on revenge and destruction.

Polly realised even her faith arrows would not stop this horde. But she remembered the other weapon the Prophet had given her. She drew the sword of truth and held it up. "Rakadan, help us!"

For an instant, nothing happened. But then, when the whites of the enemies' eyes were almost visible, a dazzling light flashed from the sword into the evil faces of the inrushing army, blinding them and causing them to halt and scatter in confusion.

Polly kept the sword in the air and looked in wonder as the light burned up the grass in front of the Nephilites and the fire drove them back. There were howls and shrieks as the giant army stumbled back, blinded by the light from the sword and harried by the fire that roared at their backs. In the end, they simply turned and ran from the battlefield.

A great cheer went up from the ranks of King Raghan's army. She heard her father call out, "Forward men!" and felt his soldiers pass her as they chased after the fleeing Nephilites. However, at that moment all she could think of was her shepherd boy who had been taken by these terrible creatures.

"Markus! Markus!" she cried out, and slumped to the ground.

CHAPTER 18
DRINKING DESTINY

When she looked up, Polly found herself in a familiar room. She saw the fire with the figures dancing and heard the heavenly music in her ears, so she guessed she was with Rakadan again. She didn't know how she had gotten there or if this was a dream, but she felt an incredible sense of peace after the excitement of the fight with the Nephilites.

Suddenly, a voice broke the silence which she recognised belonged to the Prophet: "You have done well, my child! You handled the weapons with great skill."

Polly looked up and saw Rakadan sitting at his table surrounded by scrolls and parchments. He had obviously been writing busily.

"Rakadan, they've captured Markus," said Polly tearfully. "What can we do?"

"I am just writing that, child," said the Prophet, laying down his quill.

"You ... you're writing the future?" gasped the princess.

"The future for those who will trust and obey,"

said the Prophet. "Sadly, not everyone will fulfil their destiny."

Polly gulped. "Will I?"

"That depends on you, my child."

"But what about Markus?"

Rakadan sighed. "He is a casualty of the conflict, yet you may find a way to rescue him if you are brave enough. But, it will mean going into the enemy's camp alone."

"I'll do anything to rescue Markus from those wicked things," said the princess with a most determined look.

"You must not only rescue your shepherd boy, but your people as well," said Rakadan, brandishing the scroll he had just written. "Are you willing to embrace the risk and the danger, Warrior Princess?"

"Indeed, I am," said Polly, jutting out her chin.

Rakadan took a mug from the shelf and poured some liquid from an earthenware jar, which was on the table. He then rolled the scroll up tightly and plunged it into the mug. Polly's eyes widened as she saw the scroll disappear with a hiss and green smoke rise up from the mug. Rakadan handed her the mug in which the liquid was bubbling and smoking. "This is your destiny, child. Drink this."

Polly looked at the mug and peered into the bubbling brew. She hesitated, then with a determined effort drained the contents of the mug. As she removed the cup from her lips, her face creased as if she had bitten a lemon. "Ugh! It's so bitter!"

"That is the bitterness that evil brings," said the Prophet. "But the taste will turn sweet when you have accomplished the task of vanquishing the Nephilites."

"How will I do that?"

"It is now inside you, Princess. You will know what to do. Just remember this: in your time of greatest danger, it is the arrow that flies up into the air that will bring you victory. Now go with my blessing!" Rakadan raised his hand. The next thing Polly knew, she was sitting on the ground with her brother and father standing over her.

CHAPTER 19
THE PLAN

"Polly!" cried the King with tears in his eyes, "We thought you were dead!"

He hugged his daughter tightly. "You saved us! I thought that brute was going to kill you, but you destroyed him. How on earth did you do it?"

"I had help, father," said Polly as her brother helped her to her feet, "from the old Prophet."

"Rakadan?" The King stared in amazement. "You met Rakadan?"

Polly dusted herself down. "Yes! I visited his house."

"His house?" Krennion repeated. "Where?"

Polly drew a breath and, as they were walking back to the tent, told them the story so far of how she had visited the Prophet, how he had given her the arrows and sword, and how she had gone to battle with Markus.

"Why didn't you tell us this?" asked the King as they stepped inside his tent.

"You wouldn't have believed me," said Polly. She turned to her brother. "You didn't, did you?"

Krennion looked a bit guilty, like a boy who had

been caught with his hand in the sweets jar. "No, I must admit that I didn't, Polly. But," he added, "I sure believe you now!"

He embraced his sister, at which point they were both caught up in the emotion of the moment, and cried on each other's shoulders. "To think my baby sister is a warrior!" said Krennion through his tears.

Polly stepped back and looked at her father and brother: "But the job is not yet done," she said. "We have to go and deal with the enemy, or they will be back. We must drive them off our lands once and for all and ..."

"And what?"

"Rescue the shepherd boy," said Polly.

Just then, there was a stirring outside the tent. They looked out to see the bands of soldiers who had come back from chasing the Nephilites gathered around the tent. "Hail to our Princess!" cried someone as the rest broke into spontaneous cheering and applause. They brandished their weapons and shields up and down and cried out, "Our saviour! May the Eternal Spirit bless you, Princess!"

There was quite a din, but Polly held up her hands and called for quiet. "Men," she said, "by the power of the Eternal Spirit we have won a battle. But we must win the war. The enemy has taken some of our people. We must go to their camp and get them back." She hesitated and said, "And we must drive this foul horde out once and for all, or they will return. Now—who is willing to go with me?"

There was a pause. Then a burly warrior in the middle put up his hand. He said, "I'll go with you, Princess! To the death!"

"And me!" cried another.

'Me too!"

"And me," the cries echoed as the whole force joined in.

Polly turned to her brother: "What about you?" she asked with a cheeky grin.

"You try to stop me, little sister!" He grinned as he planted a brotherly kiss on her cheek. "But where are they?"

"We'll have to find them," said the King. "But how?"

One of the soldiers came in and knelt before the King. "Your Majesty," he said, "we have captured one of the Nephilites." He pointed to where a group of soldiers were holding down a large figure.

The three royal people ran over to where the crowd was and pushed their way to the front. There on the ground being held down by four burly soldiers was a Nephilite. He was not as big as the rest of them, but still pretty huge. He actually looked fairly docile to Polly.

"Who are you?" she demanded. "Tell us."

The large creature looked at Polly with a piteous expression. "My name is Cranach," he said. "But I'm not a soldier. They say I'm too small."

"So, what are you?" asked Polly, wondering how such a huge creature could be considered too small.

"I'm a groom. I look after the nanors."

"So, you don't fight?"

"Good heavens, no. I hate fighting!" said the creature, puckering his face up.

"Why are you here then?" asked the King.

"They made me come. I live an awful life. They all bully me. Then, when that light flashed around, they trampled me and left me. I do hate being there."

Krennion laughed. "You don't seem a willing recruit."

"I'm not," said Cranach. "I just hate the sort of life we live with all the killing and looting. And I hate to see people sold as slaves, especially their children. I wish we could all just be farmers. Then I think we would be a lot happier."

"You poor thing," said Polly. "Don't you want to go back to your people, though?"

Cranach's eyes opened wide in terror. "Oh, no! They would be sure to kill me for being captured. I might get roasted over a fire for their amusement!" He looked around. "They said they were going to do it to some of you."

"Then we must find our friends who have been captured by these fiends and rescue them," said Polly. She looked at Cranach. "Can you show us where their camp is?"

"I don't know if I dare. They would do all sorts of horrible things to me if they knew!"

"There is no need for them to know," said Polly. "You can stay here with us after we have dealt with them, and live peaceably."

"That sounds wonderful," said the Nephilite with a smile. "I'll do it." He looked around as the soldiers let him up. "Without King Caspage, they will not have much of an idea about what to do. But you do need to rescue your people, or things will be really bad for them."

"We shall go tonight," said Polly, assuming command. "Cranach will lead the way and the arrows of faith and the sword of truth will destroy this evil horde."

King Raghan looked at his daughter and put his

hands on her shoulders. "Polly, this is so brave of you, but don't you think the men should go? You've done your bit and I don't want to see you hurt or killed."

Polly embraced him. "Father, I must go as I have been given the weapons that will destroy this vile rabble and drive out the evil from us. Besides, my destiny has been mapped out by the Prophet Rakadan."

"And what is that?" asked the King.

"I don't know, but I do hope the shepherd boy is a part of it," said Polly wistfully.

"Go then," said the King, "and may the Eternal Spirit be with you!"

"But you will need people to come with you," said Krennion. "We've had plenty of volunteers."

"I need just thirty men," said Polly. "Any more would alert the enemy to our coming. But make sure each man has a torch dipped in oil in each hand."

"We're going with torches?" said Krennion. "But we will be seen."

"We don't light the torches," said Polly. "They will be lit at the right moment."

"How ... What ...?" stuttered Krennion.

"Please do as I ask, dear brother," said Polly.

"You're the boss," said her brother. He went off with his father to select thirty brave men. They weren't short of volunteers, because all the men by now had fallen in love with the princess and wanted to serve her. So they selected their men carefully and the rest went about making torches with the ends soaked in oil, so they would light at the least spark. In the meantime, Polly quizzed Cranach about where the Nephilite camp would be found. She estimated that it was about a two hour march, so she decided they would set out at dusk, to arrive under cover of darkness.

According to Cranach the Nephilite custom was to spend the evening after a battle getting drunk, but that was because they always won. This time, they had been defeated, so they might have taken their hate out on Markus and the other prisoners.

An anxious look crossed the princess' face when she said, "I just hope we are in time. May the Eternal Spirit keep my shepherd boy, and the rest of my people, safe!"

CHAPTER 20
THE RESCUE

Night was falling when Polly and her brother, along with her thirty brave men, set out. King Raghan wanted to go with them, but Krennion told him that he was really getting a bit too old for this sort of thing and that he would be more of a hindrance than a help. The King was dismayed, but accepted his son's advice. Before they departed, he gave them his blessing: "You have volunteered for a dangerous mission, men, to save our people and deliver them from a great evil. Remember, however, that we do not fight alone. We have right on our side. May Rakadan and the power of the Eternal Spirit be with you."

With this, the whole camp erupted in cheers.

Raghan looked at his daughter and embraced her. "You are a true child of your mother, Polly," he said fondly. "She would have done the same. Come back safely!"

"I will, father," said Polly. "I just hope I can find my shepherd boy."

"I think you are getting very fond of him," said the

King, smiling proudly at his daughter. "Go now and bring him back!"

With Cranach leading the way, the party set out. Polly and Krennion were mounted on horses while the rest of the men were on foot. Polly felt bad about this, but Krennion insisted that she must save her energy for whatever fighting lay ahead. Besides, she had the arrows of faith and the sword of truth to carry. Before they set off, Polly had looked into the quiver and discovered that, although she had already fired three of the arrows, there were still five left. She remembered the words of the Prophet: "As long as they are used for good and in faith, there will always be five there. That is the number willed by the Eternal Spirit."

"So, these arrows really are miraculous in every way," she mused. "The Prophet was right—the Eternal Spirit really is with us."

The party travelled in silence over the hills and through some woods where the trees made weird and ghostly shapes in the moonbeams that were streaming down. Polly was glad of the moonlight as it meant finding the way would be easier, but she was anxious that it would make them more visible to the Nephilites. At last, they came to a ridge on a hill and saw a camp down below. There were various lights burning, but all seemed quiet.

"It looks as if they've been getting drunk," said Cranach, peering down at the camp. "They often do."

"Will there be any lookouts?" asked Krennion.

"Look up there," said Cranach.

As they looked, they saw two of the terrible regats with their riders circling the camp. "There are your lookouts," said Cranach.

"The question is how to get down without being seen," said Polly. "This moonlight is so bright."

Just as she spoke, the light from the moon began to dim as some clouds rolled over it. *Wow!* thought Polly. *Is this a divine intervention?*

Soon it was dark and all they could see was the glow of a few lights in the camp below. Polly whispered to Krennion, "Get the men to spread out on this ridge. When you see the light flash from my sword, tell the men to cover their eyes and hold up their torches."

"What are you going to do?" asked her brother.

"I'm going to get Markus if he's still alive, and free the other prisoners."

"But Polly, you can't go alone! Let me come with you."

"No, you'll be more useful up here."

"Please, Polly!"

"No, you'll be in the way," said the princess. "This is something I have to do on my own."

With that, Polly disappeared down the slope into the darkness, leaving her brother sick with worry. "I just hope she knows what she is doing," he muttered to himself as he went to give the men their instructions.

In the meantime, Polly slipped down the slope and was soon at the outskirts of the camp. There were several large tents which she guessed were filled with sleeping Nephilites, based on the rumbling snores she heard coming from within. She looked up and could just make out the outline of the regats flying overhead. There appeared to be no sentries on duty. Obviously the Nephilites were not expecting an attack.

She crept from tent to tent until she came to the

centre of the camp where there appeared a clearing, in the middle of which seemed to be a pile of wood. She looked closer. There, in the middle of the pile, was a figure tied to a stake. Polly gasped. It was her beloved Markus! He was slumped over and for a horrible minute she thought he was dead. However, the figure then moved his head and Polly ran over to him, climbed the wood pile and put her hand firmly over his mouth.

Markus started.

"Markus! It's me, Polly!"

"What ... what are you doing here?"

"I've come to rescue you. Are you all right?"

"Yes, I'm OK. They were pretty rough though. I've got lots of bruises. They were going to burn me alive, but all got drunk and said they'd wait till tomorrow just to prolong the agony. So, thank goodness you're here. But we're in great danger if any of these fools wake up."

Polly looked and saw three sleeping Nephilites— presumably they were supposed to be on guard, but they had nodded off. She used the sword to cut the ropes that tied Markus' wrists.

"Thanks," he whispered, "but there are more prisoners here."

"Where?" asked Polly.

"Over there."

Polly looked over in the direction Markus was pointing, and saw by the light of a torch that was burning, a sort of rough stockade made of pointed stakes. It was about ten feet high, she guessed. Two Nephilites were guarding it, but they were asleep like the rest. Markus exercised his arms and legs for a minute to get rid of the stiffness, then he and Polly climbed down the wood pile and crept to the gate of the stockade.

The gate was fixed with a rope, which Polly soon cut with her sword. Unfortunately, as she went in, a child who was sleeping woke up with a start and screamed.

"That's torn it!" said Markus.

CHAPTER 21
THE FIERY DRAGON

The guards who had been sleeping woke up and bellowed as they saw the gate open.

"What's going on?" one of them shouted as they came blundering in with drawn swords.

Polly drew her sword and pointed it at them. A bolt of lightning flashed from the point and felled the two enormous figures. But the noise had obviously disturbed the camp, and there were voices shouting and the sound of very heavy feet.

By this time, the other prisoners were awake and Polly told them quickly, "We have come to help you escape. When I raise my sword, cover your eyes. There will be a lot of confusion, but head for bright lights on the hills. Run for your lives and may the Eternal Spirit be with you!"

Polly and Markus stepped outside the stockade to find themselves surrounded by large numbers of Nephilites, some carrying torches and all at least twice the size of normal human beings. They looked hideous, even in the darkness, Polly was repulsed by them as they bellowed and threatened:

"Get them!"

"Let's roast them!"

"Yes, have an evening bonfire!"

"Kill them all!"

"Yeah, leave none of them alive!"

These and many horrible cries pierced the air, terrifying the prisoners, who began crying and wailing. Polly, however, was not afraid, but angry —angry that such evil existed. She turned furiously to the prisoners and said, "Silence! Cover your eyes!"

Then, holding the sword aloft, she cried: "In the name of Rakadan and the Eternal Spirit, let the sword of truth fight for us!"

No sooner were the words out of her mouth than light flashed from the sword into the eyes of the advancing giants who cowered back with hideous cries. She looked up and saw that the top of the ridge was lit up with fire and she guessed that the light from the sword had lit the torches held by her men. These were now burning with a light far brighter than any natural flame. *It's a supernatural blaze,* Polly thought to herself.

"Quick! Make for the light!" shouted Polly as she and Markus shepherded the helpless prisoners out of the stockade. They ran—those who could, with some helping others along—as they disappeared into the darkness towards the light.

"Come on, Polly!" said Markus.

"Just one more thing to do," said Polly as she took out an arrow.

"Look out!" said Markus. "Look what's coming!"

Polly looked and saw two of the huge regats, their bat-like wings spread out against the light, coming towards them. Polly fitted the arrow quickly and fired at one of them. The arrow lit up and sped towards its target, causing a huge explosion, completely reducing the regat and its rider to dust. The other regat veered off, then came back to attack again. Polly put another arrow in her bow, but the regat was nearly on top of them by the time she fired and the resulting explosion knocked her and Markus off their feet.

Polly sat up dizzily with the noise of the explosion ringing in her ears and the dust it had made settling around her. She looked over and saw Markus was sitting up and getting to his feet. By now, the Nephilites were beginning to recover from the blinding effect of the light and were looking up to the light coming from the ridge. Confusion reigned in the camp, but Polly knew that she must fire her arrow now before they realised what was going on.

She got to her feet, but a terrific pain in her ankle made her collapse and fall again with a cry. Markus came over and helped her up. "Are you all right?" he asked anxiously.

"Yes, but I don't think my ankle is," said Polly. "I must have twisted it when I fell." She looked at the shepherd boy. "Hold me while I fire this arrow."

"Must you? We ought to be getting away!"

"Yes, I must! Now hold me!"

Markus grasped Polly round the waist, wondering how many shepherd boys had done that to a princess, while she fitted an arrow to her bow and pointed it upwards. By this time, some of the Nephilites were coming towards them, but she drew the bow string back with her remaining strength. "The arrow that flies up into the air will bring us victory. Rakadan, help me!" she said as she released the arrow. Polly and Markus and the Nephilites near them watched as the arrow traced a fiery path into the night sky and exploded above them with a bright red flash, which lit up the whole camp and the ridge behind them.

As they looked, they saw forming in the sky the figure of a huge red dragon which glowed against the blackness of the night. It was a terrifying beast. It shook itself as if waking from a sleep, then looked down on the Nephilites with angry eyes, causing the whole camp to cry out in terror.

"Time for us to leave," said Markus.

"I can't walk!"

"Then let me carry you!" said Markus as he scooped up the princess over his shoulder. "Don't worry," he said. "I've done this with my sheep many times!" He picked up the sword that Polly had dropped and made off through the ranks of the panicking Nephilites.

Even though they were in great danger, Polly saw the humour of the moment. She wondered how many princesses had been carried over a shepherd boy's shoulder like a sack of potatoes. She reckoned if the situation had been different, she might even have enjoyed it, but then Markus wouldn't have dared to do it.

The strong shepherd boy carried his princess through the camp, the sword making a way for him with lightning flashing from the end of it, causing anyone in his way to scatter. In less than a minute, they had reached the edge of the camp and started up the hillside. Polly was full of admiration for Markus, as he didn't even break step as he climbed the hill.

Suddenly, there was a roar from the dragon. It peered at the Nephilites through its angry eyes and poured a stream of fire from its mouth towards them. The Nephilites howled and shrieked as the fire con-

THE PRINCESS AND THE SHEPHERD BOY

sumed them and everything around them. They ran in all directions, but there was no escape, especially when the dragon, for good measure, poured out another stream of molten lava from its gaping jaws. After that there was silence. All they could see by the light of the brightly glowing torches on the ledge was a gaping, smoking black hole where the camp had been. Having done that, the dragon, looked at Polly and Markus, then vanished from sight.

"Wow! It's done to them what they were going to do to us!" said Markus. "It's burned them all up!"

"Yes, the evil they have done to others has come upon them," said Polly from the vantage point of her shepherd boy's shoulder.

With that, Markus continued walking up the hillside towards the lights. He heard a voice behind him: "Markus! Put me down. I'll hop the rest of the way!"

"Not on your life! I've carried you this far and I'll carry you the rest of the way."

"But this is most undignified for a princess!"

"Tough! You're being carried. Now hold still!"

"Beast!" said Polly as she started to giggle. It did feel rather good to be carried over this strong young man's shoulder. "You wait till my ankle's better!"

"What, another wrestling match with you ending up sat on your behind?"

"Yah!" said Polly as she bounced along. Her position may have been unorthodox, but she decided she had never been so happy in all her life!

CHAPTER 22
THE RETURN OF THE HEROES

By this time, the bright lights were very near and a cheer went up from the soldiers on the bridge and from the prisoners who had escaped as Markus and Polly came into view. All sorts of excited voices cried out:

"Look, it's the shepherd boy!"

"He's alive!"

"Is that the princess with him?"

"He's rescued the princess!"

"Is she all right?"

Markus strode to the camp with Polly—now red in the face with embarrassment at her undignified position—over his shoulder. He put her into the arms of her waiting brother, then slumped to the ground with sheer exhaustion.

Krennion hugged his sister tightly. "Well done shepherd boy!" he said. "You have rescued my sister and brought her back to us. We were afraid you weren't coming back at all!"

"Actually, sir, she rescued me," said Markus. "I just carried her back because she hurt her ankle and couldn't walk."

"And in such a fashion," giggled Polly. "Just like one of his sheep!"

"Well, the main thing is that you are here," said Krennion, as the soldiers around him cheered and clapped. They helped Markus to his feet and slapped him on the back, saying, "Well done, young man! You're a hero!"

Polly looked at her shepherd boy with a look of great affection. "Oh, Markus," she said. "You were so brave!"

"But not as brave as you, Princess," said Markus. "You were the one who rescued us from those fiends!"

"Well, we won't argue about it," said Polly as she hopped over to Markus, put her arms round him, and kissed him. At this the soldiers standing around them broke into another cheer and whistled and stamped. It was all very irregular, of course, a princess kissing a shepherd boy, but no one seemed to care at that moment.

"Hurrah for the young 'uns," called out one voice, and the hurrahs rang into the night sky.

"I love you, dearest Markus," said the princess.

"I love you too," said Markus, rather awkwardly, looking into the princess' eyes.

"A princess and a shepherd boy," said Prince Krennion to himself. "I don't know how we're going to work this one out, I really don't!" He laughed heartily and joined in the cheering as loudly as anyone. Then, setting aside royal protocol, he embraced Markus like a long lost brother. "You really are a hero, shepherd boy," he said. "Thank you for saving my sister."

"An honour, sir!" said Markus.

All this time a solitary figure was looking down at where the camp had been. Polly looked and saw the huge figure of Cranach standing there, his shoulders shaking, as if he was crying.

"My people are gone!" he said. "I never liked them, but they were all I had. What shall I do now? I can't go back to the Dark Lands or they will kill me. Who will want me?"

"You can come and live with us," said Polly. "You can be one of our grooms, if you like, and take care of our horses."

"Can I really?" said the giant, his face breaking into a smile. "I'd like that!"

"We'll talk to the Queen about getting you a post," said Krennion.

"Thank you! Thank you!" said Cranach. "It makes me so happy to feel that, for the first time in my life, I am actually wanted."

And with that, the raiding party set off for the main camp. The soldiers put Polly on a horse and Markus rode behind her as they were by now totally exhausted. They also made a stretcher to drag the wounded prisoners along behind the other horse. Polly was thankful that she had her shepherd boy back. She looked into the sky. "Thank-you, Rakadan," she said.

When the party arrived at the main camp, they were greeted by a very anxious looking King Raghan who embraced his daughter tightly. Markus knelt before the King, but Raghan told him to stand up and embraced him too, not a thing a king usually did. "You are both heroes," he said. "Just what would we have done without you?"

"And what would we have done without the weapons that Rakadan gave me," said Polly. She looked at the arrows, but there were only two of them left and they did not glow as before. The sword now looked very ordinary, and even when she held it up, no light came from it. *I guess their work is done,* thought Polly, *and there is no longer the need for the magic.*

She grinned and giggled to herself: "Pity, though! Love to have tried them out at home! Just think what my sisters would have said!"

Dawn was breaking, but the rescue party were exhausted, so they settled down for a good sleep with the intention of going back home the next day. The King sent some scouts out to confirm that the Nephilites had indeed been destroyed, and when they came back, the scouts reported there was no sign of the enemy. "It appears that dragon's fire has done its work better than any of us could," said King Raghan. "We shall have a feast tonight in honour of Princess Pollinovia and the shepherd boy, Markus. And give thanks to the Eternal Spirit for our deliverance." In the meantime, he ordered the rescue party to be given tents to rest in.

Polly was so exhausted that, after taking a little refreshment of bread and wine, she fell into a deep sleep. As she slept she dreamed — or thought she dreamed — of an old man standing beside her bed. She awoke with a start to see the Prophet Rakadan standing there, his figure glowing with a light that came from within him.

"Rakadan!" she gasped.

"Well fought, Warrior Princess," he said gravely, bowing his bald head towards her. "You have fulfilled your destiny to the letter."

As Polly moved, the pain in her ankle reminded her of the very close call they had when she shot the regat. "Was nearly getting killed by that explosion part of my destiny?" she asked.

Rakadan smiled. "Our destiny sometimes involves things that can be both dangerous and painful. No one fights a war and comes out unscathed. But you have shown great courage, and have conquered a deadly foe."

"So, was the dragon a good dragon or a bad one?" Polly had been thinking about it and dying to know the answer. "I mean, was I responsible for it appearing?"

"You were responsible for delivering your people who were in great danger, Warrior Princess, by obeying the words that had been written of your destiny," said the Prophet. "The dragon represented the terrible evil that was already in the Nephilites. The arrow of faith you shot into the air in their camp simply brought the evil back on those who intended it. It burned them up." He looked intently at Polly with his piercing eyes. "There is a time when evil becomes its own destroyer!"

With that the vision — or whatever it was — vanished. The next thing Polly knew was waking up in her tent with a sore ankle.

The feast was held that night according to the King's command—a feast with such rejoicing that it had been a long time since anyone could remember such happiness. The only regret Polly had was that she couldn't stand on her ankle, so she did not join in the dancing with Markus. Speeches were made and toasts were proposed for Polly and Markus which embarrassed them no end, although they knew people were proud of them.

Celebrations were also held back in the city. The

Queen addressed her subjects when she heard the news from the King's messenger of their deliverance from the Nephilites. She ordered a time of thanksgiving to the Eternal Spirit and declared the next day a feast day. How her subjects cheered with joy and relief as the Queen moved among them, shaking hands and blessing them. She was a great hero to them, but now so was her daughter.

As for Polly's two older sisters, they were a perhaps little jealous of the attention they knew she would get and the fact that everyone would be talking about her. But they were sensible enough to put their feelings to the side as they realised that their little sister had literally saved their lives. So when the King and his party returned home, they celebrated as much as anyone else.

"Oh, Polly, just what have you done?" said Mayolinthan, hugging her. "You are so brave!"

"We're sorry we didn't believe you," said Cresethame, "but we do now! We won't doubt you again."

The celebrations went on all week with parades and street parties in honour of Polly and Markus till at last everyone felt it was time to get back to work and normality resumed. Markus went back to his sheep, but Polly continued to see him regularly when the time would allow from her royal engagements. Of course, she had now become a real celebrity and was invited around all over the place—much more, in fact, than her older sisters. But she continued to take time out to meet with Markus and to practice archery with him. Well, that was the excuse she made, anyway. The fact was that she loved being with Markus more than anyone else in the whole world!

As for the lone surviving Nephilite, Cranach, he

became a groom for the royal horses. Although the other grooms were suspicious of him at first, his good nature and cheery manner soon overcame that and he became very popular. They also found him useful as, with his great strength, he could lift a whole horse up when it needed shoeing. So Cranach lived a happy and fulfilled life, free from the bullying he'd always suffered. It was because of him the saying became known: "Even among the worst, good may be found."

But, as for Polly and her shepherd boy, there was just one problem that remained.

CHAPTER 23
THE PROPHET'S SOLUTION

"**M**other," said Polly as she entered the Queen's throne room after a meeting of state, in which the King and Queen had been consulting their counsellors, "can we have a word with you?"

The Queen looked up and noticed that Markus was also following behind the princess. Being a wise Queen, she guessed what the meeting was now going to be about.

"What is it, Polly?" said the Queen, smiling at her.

Polly shifted from foot to foot nervously, and the Queen noticed that Markus also appeared to be very nervous, even though he was dressed in a splendid robe that had been given to him to wear at the thanksgiving ceremonies.

"It's like this," said the princess. "When I first met Markus, we were just friends. But as we've gotten to know each other better, we realise we mean ... er ... we mean a lot more to each other than just that."

"What are you saying?" asked the Queen.

"Well, the fact is ..."

"Yes?"

Polly drew a deep, deep breath: "The fact is we want ... we want to be married!"

Now it was the Queen's turn to draw a deep, deep breath. She had, in fact, expected something like this to happen as she knew that her daughter and Markus were close. But a princess marrying a shepherd boy? How could such a thing be allowed?

"I'm not sure, Polly," said the Queen.

"Please, mother!"

"It would be most irregular. I mean, royalty marrying a shepherd boy!"

"No more irregular than a princess marrying a goblin," said a voice beside her.

They all looked to where the voice came from and there, standing by the window, framed against the light, stood an old man with a long white beard.

"Rakadan!" said the Queen in amazement.

"Rakadan!" repeated the King.

"Oh, Rakadan, you've come!" said Polly in a delighted voice. She ran over to the old man and kissed him impulsively. (Whether one is supposed to kiss a Prophet who lives on a mountain is uncertain, but the old man seemed pleased and smiled.)

"I was going to come before, but the sands of time prevented it. But I see you have a problem?"

"Well, yes," said the Queen. "Polly has told me she wants to marry the shepherd boy, but I cannot see how we can allow it as she is royal and he is a commoner."

"Let me help you here," said the Prophet. "First, remember that in the realm of the Eternal Spirit there is no difference between a royal person and a commoner. What counts is the heart, not the breeding."

THE PRINCESS AND THE SHEPHERD BOY

"I see," said the Queen, looking a bit chastened at the Prophet's words. "Does this mean we have to abandon our traditions?"

"We are the makers of traditions," said the Prophet with a smile. "But, in any case, you will not find it very difficult with Markus."

"Why not?" asked the King.

"Well," said the Prophet, "let's do a little family history, shall we?"

He spread his arms wide and, to the astonishment of everyone, a figure of a man appeared in front of him. It was definitely there, yet somehow not there—a bit fuzzy, like a dream, Polly thought, but she could see the man was definitely well dressed like a lord would be.

"Who is that?" asked the Queen.

"It is Lord Gwinnion," said the Prophet.

"But why ... when ...?" asked the King.

"He lived long ago," said Rakadan, "and was a noble warrior and a just ruler. But his people were driven out of their lands by raiders from the Dark Lands—the Nephilites, actually. He was killed, but his son, just a young boy, escaped with the help of a nursemaid and fled to your lands where he was adopted by a shepherd."

"A shepherd?" gasped Polly.

"And when he grew up, he married and had a family," said the Prophet, "and one of his sons became Markus' father."

"So ... so my great-grandfather was a lord?" said Markus, looking quite bewildered. "How come I never knew this?"

"Your grandfather never actually knew of his background as he was very young when he was brought here," said Rakadan. "He always thought he was the son of the shepherd. And no one told him, for fear of what he might do if he found the Nephilites had taken his land. They wanted him to live peacefully as a shepherd, which he did. But now the Nephilites are no longer a threat, there is no reason that it should be kept a secret."

"So, Markus is descended from a lord," said Polly, her face lighting up. "He is noble?"

"Yes, my child," said the Prophet, smiling. "He is descended from nobility. So, you can be married to Markus and your mother can still keep her royal traditions intact."

Then turning to the Queen, he said, "I suggest you restore to Markus the lands his family lost. They have been liberated since the Nephilites have been destroyed." Then, looking at Markus, he said, "I think they will be glad to have a wise and caring lord to watch over them." Then looking at Polly, he added, with a twinkle in his eye, "And of course his lady princess."

"Excellent!" said the Queen, bowing her head to the Prophet. Turning to Polly, who now had Markus by her side, she said, "We know that the wisdom of the Prophet Rakadan brings the blessing of the Eternal Spirit when we obey. So, here is my command: that the Lord Markus' lands be restored to him and that they be always linked to our realm through his marriage to the Princess Pollinovia."

"How wonderful!" said Polly, as she and Markus embraced. "Thank-you Rakadan ..." But when she turned to where the Prophet had been, she saw that he had disappeared. "He's gone back to that golden

THE PRINCESS AND THE SHEPHERD BOY

mountain of his, I suppose," she murmured. "But what is that?"

On the table next to where the Prophet had been standing was what looked like a wooden box, except that the lid appeared to be glowing and sparkling in the light coming from the window. Polly walked over to it and saw there were words on the lid that appeared to be alive, as they winked and flickered at her. When she made out the words, they said: *"For the wedding of the Warrior Princess."* Polly opened the box and looked inside and gasped. It was a beautiful gold ring.

CHAPTER 24
A VERY HAPPY UNION

The wedding of Princess Pollinovia and Lord Markus took place amid great rejoicing and feasting. Her sisters acted as the bridesmaids and Prince Krennion (who was by now firm friends with Markus) was the master of ceremonies for the occasion. The princess looked radiant as Markus slipped the ring the Prophet had given her on her finger. As he did so, she felt a strange warmth come over her and felt the same power in her that she'd felt in her meetings with Rakadan. As she looked up, she thought she saw right through the ceiling. There, high above her, was the Prophet giving them his blessing.

They said goodbye to their families and journeyed to the lands Markus had inherited. The people were glad to have a royal princess - the daughter of the Queen herself - and her husband as their rulers. So, there was a great celebration when Polly and Markus arrived.

The people of the land were very poor, because they had been slaves of the Nephilites and had nothing of their own. They had only avoided starvation by planting crops and keeping a few animals.

However, because Polly and Markus had carried with them the blessing of the Eternal Spirit, the land began to prosper again. One of the things Markus did was set up sheep farms, and after a time there were literally thousands of sheep chewing the rich grass. Poverty became a thing of the past and people forgot the terrible times when they were slaves of the Nephilites.

To celebrate the anniversary of Polly's triumph over the Nephilite King, Queen Aavantar set up an archery contest which was to be held every year. It was known as *"The Royal Archery Contest Celebrating the Triumph of Her Royal Highness, Princess Pollinovia, over the Nephilite Invaders."* That was a bit of a long winded title, so the people simply called it *"Princess Polly's Archery Contest"*. An archery competition was held in all six realms of the kingdom and the winner of each came to the palace for the final to decide the greatest archer in the kingdom that year.

This gave Polly and Markus the chance to come home and see their families as, of course, Polly had to be there to present the prize in the presence of the Queen. The prize given out was always the same—a mounted replica of one of the arrows of faith. On the plinth was inscribed the name of the winning archer and the simple words: *"Have Faith"*.

These words were Markus' idea, as he reckoned that it was through Polly's faith in the words of Rakadan and the power of the Eternal Spirit that the people had been rescued from a fate worse than death. Of course, in doing so the princess also won the hand of the person she loved best—her beloved shepherd boy. Needless to say, they lived happily ever after!

Dear reader,

We hope you enjoyed reading *The Princess and the Shepherd Boy*. Please take a moment to leave a review, even if it's a short one. Your opinion is important to us.

Discover more books by David Littlewood at https://www.nextchapter.pub/authors/david-littlewood

Want to know when one of our books is free or discounted? Join the newsletter at http://eepurl.com/bqqB3H

Best regards,

David Littlewood and the Next Chapter Team

ABOUT THE AUTHOR

David Littlewood is a freelance speaker, author and writer, whose travels have taken him to many countries all over the world. A prolific writer, he has contributed and edited many articles for a variety of publications over the years, and is the author of a number of books, including historical biographies, together with novels for children of all ages. Titles include Ghastly Gob Gissimer, Ava and the Goblin Prince, The Princess and the Shepherd Boy, Jedrek and the Pirate Princess and Gary and the Granny-Bot.

David has been married to Hilda for over 50 years, with two children and four grandchildren. When not writing, David's interests include classical music, cricket and rugby union, although, he hastens to add, in a spectator capacity only!

NOTES

1. THE IRREGULAR PRINCESS

1. Read the story in 'Ava and the Goblin Prince' by David Littlewood

3. A LESSON IN ARCHERY

1. See 'Ava and the Goblin Prince' by David Littlewood

5. THE SCOLDING

1. A bowyer is someone who makes bows for archers

7. THE ATTACK OF THE WALVERATS

1. A quiver is a case for holding and carrying arrows

The Princess And The Shepherd Boy
ISBN: 978-4-82410-836-4
Mass Market

Published by
Next Chapter
1-60-20 Minami-Otsuka
170-0005 Toshima-Ku, Tokyo
+818035793528

7th October 2021

www.ingramcontent.com/pod-product-compliance
Lightning Source LLC
LaVergne TN
LVHW032012070526
838202LV00059B/6420